MURDER ON ICE

MURDER ON ICE

Ted Wood

CHARLES SCRIBNER'S SONS • NEW YORK

Also by Ted Wood
Dead in the Water

Copyright © 1984 Ted Wood

Library of Congress Cataloging in Publication Data

Wood, Ted.
  Murder on ice.

  I. Title.
PR9199.3.W57M8   1984   813'.54   84–1298
ISBN 0–684–18134–7

1 3 5 7 9 11 13 15 17 19   F/C   20 18 16 14 12 10 8 6 4 2

Printed in the United States of America.

For my mother,
who taught me the value of words

———•———

Now everybody who
buys the book will
know how much I
owe you.
With love and
gratitude

Ted.

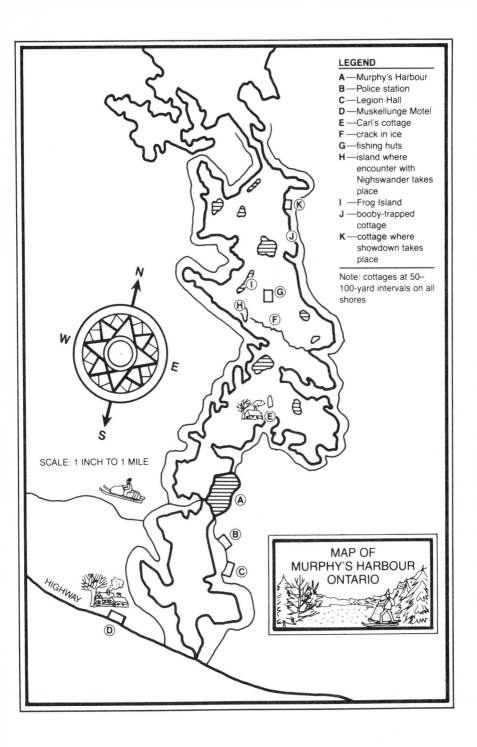

LEGEND

A —Murphy's Harbour
B —Police station
C —Legion Hall
D —Muskellunge Motel
E —Carl's cottage
F —crack in ice
G —fishing huts
H —island where encounter with Nighswander takes place
I —Frog Island
J —booby-trapped cottage
K —cottage where showdown takes place

Note: cottages at 50–100-yard intervals on all shores

N
W   E
S

SCALE: 1 INCH TO 1 MILE

HIGHWAY

MAP OF
MURPHY'S HARBOUR
ONTARIO

1

A kid in a mackinaw jacket stumbled out of the fire door of the Lakeside Tavern and collapsed against the six-foot snowdrift under the emergency light. I watched from the police car as he rolled onto one elbow and pried himself erect, one hand cupped over his mouth. Blood oozed between his fingers, black in the yellow light.

I opened the car door and stepped out, calling Sam to heel. He jumped out and followed me along the shoveled walkway between the man-high walls of snow, through the thin new snow that was driving almost flat against my face on the bitter northeast wind. The kid was reeling but I judged he was more drunk than hurt.

I grabbed him by the elbow and he took down his hand and gaped at me, trying to focus his eyes. He was short a couple of front teeth but this is hockey country, he could have lost them years earlier. I told him, "Come inside, you'll freeze out here." I let go of his elbow and he followed, docile as Sam, around to the main door and through the lobby to the low-ceilinged cocktail lounge, following the sounds of the fight. It was still going on at the far end of the room, on the other side of a wall of locals who were whooping and cheering, standing on tiptoe or on chairs to get a look. Most of them were nickel miners and bush-workers, tougher than any city crowd. But I had Sam.

I told him "Speak!"

He fell into his snarling, barking crouch, stiff legged and savage. He's a big black and tan German Shepherd with one ear torn away in an old battle. It gives him a lopsided ugliness that makes people step aside. The crowd parted and we went through. Somebody shouted, "It's the cops!" and I felt the old wry amusement. Sure! The whole Murphy's Harbour contingent—Reid Bennett and Sam.

The standard bar fight has two men in work shirts swinging big sucker punches at one another or sometimes working on one another with steel-toed safety boots. This was different. Neither man was swinging. One was a local, a truck driver for the nickel mine. He runs into the States and figures he's a hard case. But tonight he was scared. He was in a crouch holding a chair in front of him, light in his big hands. His opponent was the wild card in the game. He was tall and elegant, dressed in a velour shirt and expensive corduroy pants. He was circling silently on the balls of his feet, his hands up in the classic karate pose.

The trucker shot me an appealing glance but I didn't respond. Most Friday nights when I come here, he's standing over some drunk, usually smaller or older than he is. Tonight he had picked wrong and I wanted him to sweat a little.

Finally I told Sam "Easy" and he switched off like a radio, standing, watching the two men, ready to leap as soon as I asked.

The trucker's wife was drunker than usual. She hadn't grasped what was happening. In the sudden silence her shout was shrill. "Garrrn! Kick his goddamn teeth in!"

The karate man lowered his hands. He had nothing to fear from the trucker, chair or no chair. Slowly, keeping safely behind his chair, the trucker lowered it and backed off. His wife had noticed me now and she shouted, "Them sonsabitches picked on Harry."

2

I said nothing, studying the karate man. He was narrow and dried out, with a dancer's build and the studio-tanned, young-old face you see on a lot of gay men. I judged him to be around my age, thirty-five. I had never seen him before. There were two others like him in the crowd, one his age, one younger. They were behind him, on the edge of the crowd.

The trucker began to bluster. "He kicked my bro'r in the mouth. Waddya gonna do about that?"

He knew the answer. He'd heard me give the instructions to his own victims. I ignored him. Instead I turned to the karate man.

"I know these other people, they live here. Could I have your name, please?"

He took out his billfold and flipped it open at the driver's license. I read his name, George Nighswander, and an address in Toronto. I could tell from the coded number on his chauffeur's license that he was thirty-six.

"I didn't start this," he said, speaking softly.

The trucker, whose name I remembered to be Cassidy, shouted immediately but kept his distance. I let him shout, speaking to Nighswander. "I'm not concerned with causes. All I need is your name and address in case one of them wants to lay an assault charge. Aside from that, you're free to go."

He ducked his head and said, "Thank you, officer."

Cassidy was still fuming but feeling safe now, with Sam and me there to protect him. He ducked his own head, mimicking Nighswander. "Thank you, officer!" he lisped, then spat and said, "Goddamn fruit!"

Nighswander closed his billfold and pushed it back into his hip pocket. I asked him, "What brings you this far north, Mr. Nighswander?" I kept my voice polite. After all, he had the right to be anywhere he wanted, even two hundred miles north of Toronto with its gay bars and steam baths.

"I'm here with friends for the Winter Carnival," he said primly. "We were having a quiet drink and this man began

3

making personal comments. I didn't like it and said so, and his associate tried to punch me."

"And you retaliated?"

He nodded. Good! I thought. It might discourage Cassidy from picking fights, even with strangers in soft clothes who look as out of place in Murphy's Harbour in January as a bird of paradise in a chicken run.

I turned to the kid with the broken mouth. He was standing where I had left him, blood still dripping through his fingers.

"You've heard this man's name. If you want to lay a charge, go to the Justice of the Peace on Monday and swear out a warrant." He blinked a couple of times, painfully, and gave a slow nod. He would lay no charges. He was beaten and he knew it. So did Cassidy, but he was anxious to save face in front of the crowd. They would never again fear him, not now.

"There's other ways to settle this," he said suddenly.

"Maybe Mr. Nighswander will oblige you," I told him. "If you're bound and determined to fight, go outside and finish it now." It's not the speech a policeman is supposed to make, but I'm alone in this town and I sometimes cut corners.

Cassidy swore and turned away from me to his wife. "Screw this place. Let's get the hell home."

She was a big tough bottle blonde who had once worked as a cook in bush camps. She liked fights. "Are you gonna let that pansy get away with it?" she shouted. The crowd laughed and cheered and Cassidy's face grew redder than usual. "Shut your yap," he hissed. "You started this mess." He picked up his parka, said "Let's go," and left, brushing insolently close to Nighswander, who stepped aside gracefully and made a mocking little *maitre d'* gesture.

That was the end of it. All three Cassidys went, and the visitors gathered at one table while the rest of the crowd settled back to its beer. I waited another minute, then nodded a signal to Sam and went to the bar. The barman flipped up the flap on the counter, winking at me. I winked back and went down the corridor to Irv Whiteside's office. Irv's the manager but he's never in his office on Friday. That's the night he brings in a girl from Toronto. They have the surf 'n' turf dinner while the crowd gets a good look at her, then he takes her upstairs. It's one of his vanities, making the isolated bush-workers drool with envy. That's why he always brings girls in for the weekends in winter. Summertimes he finds companionship from the tourists and cabin renters.

The waitress came in after me, flashing buck teeth as she snapped her gum. "Hey, thanks, Chief. You wanna talk to the boss?"

"When he comes down. No panic."

"Okay." She stopped the sentence with a snap of her gum. "You like your usual?" My reward for acting as tavern bouncer. I thanked her and she went for the Black Velvet. Policemen aren't supposed to drink on duty, but I'm the only member of the force so I'm never off duty and I never have more than a single shot.

I stood at the door of the office and watched the crowd again. Everyone was settled down except for one overfriendly near-drunk who was talking to Nighswander. The two men with Nighswander were grinning at one another, probably at the ignorance of the local. I decided I didn't like any one of them.

I wondered again why they were here. Our little Winter Carnival isn't important enough to draw strangers from Toronto, and I didn't recognize any of the men as cottagers. They were not the cottage type, anyway. They didn't look like family men. If they wanted sunshine they would go to the Club Med somewhere or buy themselves sun lamps. Automatically, I filed their descriptions in my memory.

Irv came in as I was sipping my whisky. He's my height,

six feet one, but a lot thicker, and his face has the smudginess of a failed fighter. He was a contender once, light-heavyweight, but took enough beatings to quit and find an easier line of work. He broke legs for a loan shark in Montreal, was arrested once but never convicted. I may be the only person in the Harbour to know that about him. Local gossip pegs him as a former mob hit man and he basks in it. He's in his early forties and he was wearing a dove-gray suit with a light pink shirt and a black tie.

He said, "Hi, Reid, Isabelle take care of you?" I raised my shot glass in salute. "Yeah, thanks, Irv." He nodded toward his office and we went in and sat down, him behind the desk with the signed picture of the last fighter to beat him, me on the chesterfield that took up the length of the wall.

"Ever seen those three city guys before?"

"Which three?"

I explained and he shook his head, doing a little negative thing with the corners of his mouth. "Don't ring a bell with me. I guess they're here for the Carnival." I finished the last warm drop of rye. "Wonder where they heard about it. They don't look like cottagers."

Nobody else would have known. Our Carnival was too small to have been written up in the Toronto papers. We had no sponsors, we weren't raising money for charity. We would not have reached the attention of a gang of trendies.

Irv wasn't bothering about the three men. He was thinking about women, his constant preoccupation as far as I could tell. He grinned at me. "You gonna be a judge at the beauty contest?"

I shook my head. "No. But don't think I'm crying. I can make enough enemies just doing my job, without playing favorites with local girls."

I don't think he heard me. He was so full of his own information. "I know who's gonna win. I just wish I could get a bet down, that's all."

"Yeah, who's that?" I knew the names of the few local girls who had entered. Each was pretty but sturdy—there wasn't a clear winner among them.

Irv leaned across his desk confidentially. "Nancy Carmichael. You know, the big yellow cottage up near the north lock, that's her folks' place."

"I didn't realize any summer people were entering."

Irv nodded, still grinning. "Neither did I, but she is. And she's got it all over them other broads like a rash. Like, she's rich, eh? She took one o' them modeling courses in T'rannah an' on top of that, she's . . ." He gave up trying to find words and sketched curves in the air.

"You sound like she's waiting upstairs for you right now."

"I wish," he sighed. "She's up there, her an' her folks, but they're only stayin' here because it's closer to the Legion. Her old man's gotta heart problem. He didn't want the hassle of opening their place up in the cold."

I stood up and set down my glass on his desk top. "I'm glad you told me. I promised the Reeve I'd drop by the Carnival and see everything's in order. Now I can get to see Miss Rich Kid. It makes the whole thing worthwhile."

He stood up with me, grinning his meaty, pool-hall hustler grin. "Do yourself a favor, Reid. I mean, this kid's got everything."

2

It was snowing hard when I left the Lakeside. There was already a crust over the cars, and small sharp flakes stung my face.

I scraped the windows of the scout car, wondering how many people would turn out for the Carnival dance. This is inhospitable country in January. In the old days before electric light, men lost their way between their back doors and their woodsheds on nights like this and died of exposure. Sensible people stay indoors.

But this was no normal night. Murphy's Harbour makes its living from the Toronto people and the Americans who swarm north to our lake in July and August. The rest of the year, the locals take day jobs or draw unemployment. The Reeve wants to change that. He wants people up here in winter as well, snowmobiling and buying their food and propane and gas and firewood from the locals. That's why he started this Winter Carnival. He's smart enough to realize that bad weather can be an attraction. I saw the invitation he'd sent to our cottage owners. He told them that the Legion Hall would be equipped to keep everyone safe and sound overnight if a blizzard blew up. By that he probably meant they would keep extra liquor on hand so everyone could feel good about losing a night's sleep. It would probably mean a full house.

Maybe most of them would have stayed in the city if they had expected really bad weather, but this snow had been forecast only this morning. Most people who had planned to come for the weekend would still turn up. I guessed that quite a few of them would be stuck in the Legion Hall overnight.

My own plan was to make a formal appearance, shake a few hands, and pick up my date, a woman called Val Summers from Toronto. She's the widow of a policeman I'd worked with there. I met her once when he was alive, but I'd slowly worked up to a real friendship over the last few months on my trips to the city. Now she had left her two boys with their grandmother and was coming up to stay with me for the weekend. She was meeting me at the dance and then we would head back to my place with its warm wood stove.

The Legion parking lot was almost full. Many of the cars were snowed in, a sign that they had been there for an hour or so. Here and there among the parked cars were snow-mobiles. Most people up here call them skidoos, which was the name of the original Canadian invention, but nowadays there are a dozen models, many of them made in Japan. If the snow kept on all evening, they might be the only way to come and go from the Legion by midnight.

The only other noticeable vehicles in the lot were a van with a psychedelic paint job and a Toyota four-wheel drive. The van was parked in front of the hall, illegally. I guessed it belonged to the disc jockey, a guy from Parry Sound, our nearest city. The Toyota was standing at the end of a row of parked cars. I imagined the occupants were playing kissy-face and debating whether to go to the dance or head home for something more strenuous.

I parked the scout car behind the DJ's van and went into the hall. It's the standard small-town Legion. There's a lobby with a soaking coconut mat where people kick off their snow boots. It's hung with pictures—the Queen, of course, and photographs of parades with old or middle-aged men wearing ribbons they had won in Europe or Korea. They had asked me to be part of the show because I served in Nam with the U.S. Marines, but I'm not anxious to commemorate any killing I did then, or since.

I went up the single step to the double doors. An old Legionnaire was sitting inside at a card table that held dance tickets, liquor tickets, and the inevitable bottle of Molson Export Ale. He grinned, "Hi, Chief. Just in time for the beauty contest."

"Naturally," I said, and we both grinned again. I glanced around and got my first surprise of the occasion. Everyone in the hall was wearing a mask.

"Whose idea was the masks?"

He shrugged. "Some broad, kind of skinny. She was wearing one when she came in, gave me the box, and asked to give one to everybody, so I did."

I nodded acknowledgment and walked around the edge of the floor to the office, Sam a neat six inches from my left heel. Walter Puckrin was sitting at a table counting money. He's the man who runs the marina, the biggest industry in town. He's a big, heavy guy in his sixties. He won a gallantry medal on his destroyer on the Murmansk run during the war. A useful guy to know. There was a bottle of cheap rye on the table. The top was off and lying beside it, a sign that he intended to finish the jug before he'd finished celebrating this evening.

He waved me to sit down. "Hi, Reid. Tonight's the night."

"For what?"

He gestured at the money in front of him. "For payin' off the mortgage on this place. Lookit. Three hundred and eighty-four dollars a'ready and we'll take another three hundred easy from the bar."

"*Mazel tov,*" I said, and he chuckled.

"If that means good luck, thanks. Like a snort?"

"No thanks, I'm up to capacity. Mind if I leave Sam in here? It'll save him from being fussed by the crowd, and he'll look after your cash."

"Help yourself," he said amiably, and poured another slug of Special Old. I told Sam "Stay" and he settled down on the floor.

I stood in the doorway a minute or two, watching people who were old enough to know better doing the twist to Bill Haley's "Rock around the Clock." With the masks pulled down over their eyes they all looked like Lone Rangers, but I soon picked out the figure I was watching for. There's no mistaking Val Summers—she's tall, dark haired, and graceful. It would take more than a mask to disguise her from me.

She finished twisting when the record ended, and came over to me. "Hi, Reid. I made it."

"Nice going. Want to hang around for a while longer?" She was dressed for dancing, a mid-length number that must have cost her a week's pay. But she laughed. "I didn't get off work at four and drive two hundred miles in this weather to boogaloo."

"Great. I just have to hang around until the contest is over, in case somebody gets fresh with the talent."

"Pervert. You just want an eyeful of that young stuff." She pushed the mask up on top of her head and winked at me. "I'll mingle till you're ready." She mouthed an almost invisible kiss and turned away. I couldn't help smiling at her cheerfulness. But she hasn't always been that way. Three years ago her husband answered a radio call to a domestic dispute. He knocked on the door and the common-law husband inside answered with a twelve-gauge shotgun blast through the glass. Val was twenty-seven then, with two boys to raise. It's taken her a long time to get her sense of humor back. It was good to see her enjoying herself and I was glad I'd invited her up here.

I watched while the dance went on for another few

minutes, then the disc jockey played a little fanfare and the dancers stopped. The Reeve came out on stage. He's our township's elected officer, a short guy who runs the real estate office. He was wearing the only tux to be found within a hundred miles of Murphy's Harbour and he was loving himself.

"Welcome!" he said, waving his arms like the Pope blessing the multitudes. "Welcome to the second annual Murphy's Harbour Winter Carnival." There was some clapping and calling out and he went on to explain what was happening over the next couple of days. It was the routine stuff for these occasions. Snowmobile races on the lake. Snowshoe races. A dog-sled race between a couple of teams pulled together by the local Indians from the pack of mutts on the Reserve. The ice sculptures on Main Street would be judged and there would be an ice-fishing derby. And of course, a parade of floats and snowmobiles, headed by the winner of the beauty pageant.

The whistling started here. Everything was happy and small town and cheerful. The Reeve milked it, telling us he had assembled the finest judges of beauty to be found in the area and that they were ready to begin.

Before he could finish, Carl Simmonds, the local photographer, took the microphone and resigned from the committee. Carl is the town's only obvious homosexual. He had to make a sparse living here at best, and I often wondered why he stayed in a place as quiet as this. But he's a good man and a good photographer who has helped me out on a couple of cases. He announced that all the young women were so lovely that he wouldn't presume to pick one above the others, and bowed out. He got down from the stage and prepared to pay for his evening, setting up a tripod with one camera on it, hanging another camera and his meters around his neck.

The rest of the panel formed up, big, hearty men, taking heavy ribbing from their wives, and the contest began. The

12

girls paraded out on stage in swimsuits. There were eight of them. Seven were local girls, the other was Nancy Carmichael. I guessed that at once. She had a rich girl's prettiness and all the grace that money and training could provide.

They circled once while the audience cheered and whistled. Then they moved to center stage, one by one. The local girls did their best, moving with their own innate grace and any skills they might have picked up from watching actresses on TV. Then Nancy Carmichael came to center stage, one foot drawn up behind her the way she must have been taught. She smiled down into our eyes, did the things with her lips that models do in hair-care commercials, and it was all over but the crowning.

The Reeve spun it out as long as he could, collecting ballots and comparing, going from one side of the stage to the other, milking his moment. Then he straightened up at the microphone and said, "Ladies and gentlemen, I give you the Queen of the Carnival, Miss Murphy's Harbour." He turned and placed the crown on Nancy's head.

In the instant before the crowd could applaud, every light in the hall went out.

I stayed where I was, against the wall, listening to the crowd murmur and feeling in my parka pocket for the flashlight I carry. I felt a blast of cuttingly cold air sweep into the room. A woman screamed, but, astonishingly, there was a brief whoop of laughter before a flash from Carl's camera equipment went off. In the afterglow it left in my eyes I read the scene like a snapshot. The Reeve was standing with his mouth open and no words coming out. The judges and disc jockey were turned, facing the back of the stage, the also-ran girls were standing in their line to one side. But the Carnival Queen had vanished.

3

Not even stopping to whistle Sam I plunged toward the lobby, bumping people on the dance floor but finding the door first try as I pulled out my flashlight. The outside door was shut and I threw myself against the one I had opened on my way in. It stopped me dead, slamming my face against the wood. I flashed my light through the crack and saw that somebody had wedged a two-by-four timber through the big handles outside. For a moment I considered drawing my gun and blasting it away, but I didn't. Someone could be in the line of fire, and if this was just a prank I didn't want a corpse on my conscience.

I went back into the hall, keeping to the near wall, using my light. I whistled for Sam and in a moment he was behind me. There is a gap between wall and stage and I went along it to the fire door behind. Carl's flash went off a few more times but I kept going. The pictures would be useful later, if I was lucky. In the meantime I still had a chance to catch the kidnappers outside.

I hit the outside door more respectfully this time, pushing the fire bar down with one hand. It gave without trouble and I plunged out into a waist-deep snowdrift. I floundered down the side of the hall, in footsteps that were new and crisp. Sam bounded after me, rising and falling in the snow. By now I was at least thirty seconds behind Nancy Carmichael and whoever was with her and I called "Track" to Sam. He pushed harder, passing me, forcing himself forward, giving tongue like a hound.

I reached the corner of the building a couple of seconds after him and saw him bounding over the cleared snow in the parking lot toward the Toyota I'd noticed earlier. It was moving away, gathering speed as it slipped down the open stretch in front of the hall toward the gateway.

I shouted "Stop!" but the wind tore the words out of my mouth and flung them sideways with the driven snow. I grabbed automatically for the gun in my right pocket but by the time I had it clear there were ninety feet between me and the vehicle, so I lowered it. This could be a gag of some kind and that is not a capital offence. I swore once and sprinted for the scout car, stuffing the gun back into my holster pocket and calling Sam, but as I reached it I could see it was too late. The tires were flat, all four of them.

The Toyota side-slipped as it went out of the parking lot and I waited to see if it would go off the road but it corrected and headed south toward the highway. I hadn't been able to read the license number even earlier. It had been snow-covered and now I wondered if that had been deliberate.

The two-by-four in the front door was easy to dislodge. I threw it to one side in a snowdrift. Maybe later I would fingerprint it. Probably whoever had handled it was wearing gloves but it was all I had so far.

The lights came on in the hall as I found my way back in. The place was in an uproar. Men and women were milling about, shouting and arguing. The Reeve was shouting into the microphone which came back to life with a sudden feed-back scream. Walter Puckrin was on his feet, looking about himself angrily, like a sacked quarterback. His money was

15

untouched. Before he could say anything I said, "Gimme your keys, Walt, somebody's slashed the tires on the scout car."

He dug out his keys and wondered out loud what the hell was going on. I said, "Later. The kid's missing. Where are you parked?" He told me and I ran out, shouting "Thanks" over my shoulder. I paused to speak to the Legionnaire at the door. "Don't let anybody leave. I'll be back as soon as I can."

He started to bluster but I cut him off. "I'll leave Sam in the lobby. That'll hold them this end of the building, anyway."

I pushed through and told Sam "Keep." He stopped and settled down on the mat, looking over his new area of responsibility.

Puckrin's Blazer was covered with snow, but I started it away without waiting. Enough snow fell off under the wipers that I was able to keep going. The outside mirror was covered but that didn't bother me. Nothing would overtake me for the next few minutes. I had no trouble chasing the twin ruts left by the Toyota. The inside of the windshield began to mist and I frantically wiped it clear so I could see ahead, through the funneling snowflakes that threw themselves down the beam of the headlights.

I was grateful to be following ruts. The roadbed was obliterated by snow. From time to time I made out a marker post beside the roadbed but otherwise I followed the tracks, making better time than the first guy had, I was sure of that. But I also knew that whoever was driving the Toyota knew the road like the back of his hand, better than I do and I've worked here almost a year. If he hadn't, he would have spun out onto the lake that lay below the right shoulder.

As I drove I made sure there were no trampled areas beside the ruts. Nobody had gotten out of the vehicle. I glanced up at the few cottages on this stretch of road but they were all in darkness. I pressed harder on the accelerator.

The Toyota was heading for the highway. Once it got there, it had gotten away.

I rounded the last bend before the stop sign and saw a two-foot pile of snow across the road, left by the highway plow. The driver had ignored the whole of Murphy's Harbour, just cut us off rather than lift his blade as he passed our corner on the highway. And then I saw the Toyota, abandoned at roadside, just ahead of the drift, one door hanging open.

I pulled up right behind it, my headlights shining through the back window which was covered already with a skim of snow. Even before I got down from the Blazer I knew it was too late. The vehicle was empty. I stopped and checked the footprints around it. Three people had left, two from the passenger side. The prints were clear and there was no sign of a struggle. By stooping and checking closely with my flashlight I could make out that two sets were boot prints and the others had been made by small high-heeled shoes. I straightened up, a little less anxious now. The Carnival Queen had gone as she was on stage. And she had gone without a struggle.

I checked the Toyota's interior. It was empty except for a strong smell of perfume. Then I turned and followed the footprints thirty yards ahead, over the drift and onto the shoulder of the highway. The prints stopped there, at three points where the doors would be on a car—a domestic make of some kind, judging by the distance between the wheel tracks. I could tell the car had been waiting a few minutes. There was more snow in the tracks behind it than there was in those in front. It had headed north but it didn't make any sense to climb the drift in the Blazer and try to follow. The tracks vanished almost immediately on the smoothly plowed surface of the highway. For all I knew, the car could have made a U-turn anywhere and headed south again, down the same single-width track plowed out by the Highways Department.

It was time for a little slow and steady police work. I checked the license number on the Toyota and then headed back to the Legion Hall. There was a chance that the girl was still there, hidden under the stage or somewhere. Sam would find her in seconds, given a sniff of the clothes she had left behind when she changed into her swimsuit. And if she wasn't, I might learn something from the photographs Carl Simmonds had taken or perhaps from him directly. He has a good eye for detail, I've found that out before. He might have seen someone he recognized in the light from his flash.

I steered clear of the Toyota's tracks in the parking lot, getting out to check them. It was easy to see where the car had been parked before it took off. The footprints came right up to it. There were two sets, one of a small boot and the other of high heels. No woman in her right mind would wear high heels outside on a night like this except in an emergency. It must have been the Carnival Queen. My reading was that Snowboots had waited at the fire door in the hall, possibly inside. Probably she had a coat for the missing girl. They had cut and run as soon as the lights went off. The getaway vehicle was driven by a third person.

Sam sprang to his feet as I entered the lobby and I rubbed his big head and told him "Come" as I pushed the inner door open.

At first I thought a fight had started. The crowd had gathered around one corner of the stage, pushing and craning to see what was going on. A couple of women were screaming but I saw other women turning away, disgusted. One of them saw me and shouted, "Arrest her! It's filthy!"

Sam spoke on command and the crowd opened for us, onto the most surprising sight of the evening so far. A young thin woman, almost pathetically plain, was standing in front of the stage dressed only in a flat white brassiere and panties of a serviceable cut. She was holding up a card which read: "Down with Male Chauvinism. Long live the C.L.A.W."

18

4

She was almost hysterical, shouting the slogan on her banner over and over in a high cracking voice that told me she was scared. Sam added to the terror. She tried to ignore him but he came within an inch of her thin legs, still barking, slavering. She drew back and back until she was flat up against the stage.

I glanced around. All the men were watching hungrily, plain as she was. Their masks were shoved up on their heads so they could have an unobstructed view. Most of them were grinning like schoolboys.

I touched the closest man on the shoulder. "Lend me your jacket, please." He slipped it off, puzzled, and handed it to me. I said, "Thanks. Easy, Sam." People started shouting again as soon as Sam was quiet and the girl waved her piece of paper and went on chanting. I tossed her the jacket. She caught it reflexively with her left hand. "Put it on, you'll catch cold," I told her.

She stared at me blankly, as if she were coming out of a trance, then began to shiver. She slipped her arms into the jacket sleeves, clamping her banner between her knees in a gesture that was pure Charlie Chaplin. While she held it there I could read the bottom line that I hadn't noticed before. It was *Canadian League of Angry Women.*

Up on stage the Reeve was booming away and I looked up and shook my head. Then I nodded to the DJ and made a little conducting gesture with my hands. He read me and put some rock record on his machine. I touched the girl on the elbow and led her away toward Puckrin's office. The crowd stood back, the way a hockey crowd does when a player goes to the dressing room to have stitches put in his head.

Walter Puckrin was at the door, blocking it with his body, protecting the Legion money. He stood aside and the girl went in dejectedly. Her head was hanging and all her venom and energy had drained away. She looked deflated, like prisoners you see in newspaper photographs of trials.

Val Summers came out of the crowd, her mask pushed up on her head like a perched butterfly. She was carrying a bundle of clothes. I nodded to her and she followed the girl and me into the office and shut the door. She handed me the clothes.

"I guess these are hers. They were around the edge of the stage."

"Thanks." I turned to the girl. "Put these on, please." Walter opened his mouth to say something but I said, "We'll wait outside while she dresses. Mrs. Summers will keep an eye on your money." He shook his head disbelievingly and followed me out. We stood with our backs to the door, ignoring the questions from the crowd.

Carl Simmonds came up to me, excited. "I think I got a shot of somebody in outdoor clothes, at the back of the stage. I'm going home to print it up for you. I'll call here when it's done."

"Try the station first, I may be down there with this prisoner. And thanks, Carl."

He left a moment later. Val opened the office door and handed me the suit coat. "You can come in now."

I handed the jacket back to its owner and went back in.

20

Putting some clothes on had made the girl less unattractive. She looked almost pretty in her green skirt and soft white blouse. "That's better," I said. A policeman has to be a father figure sometimes, it softens people up to answer questions.

Walter started to bluster something but I caught his eye and he stopped, bending instead to recount his money. I stood looking at the girl for perhaps thirty seconds, wondering if she would start to speak and give anything away but she stayed grimly silent, looking at me and then away, being brave. I realized what I would have to do. It's a bit less than legal, but it was the only move that made sense.

"Tell me your name, please?"

All she said was, "Fascist!"

"Have it your own way." I turned to Val, dropping her the shadow of a wink. "Mrs. Summers, I am about to arrest this person. We have no matron on staff at Murphy's Harbour. I'm asking you to volunteer to stay with her until she is locked up. I don't want any false accusations made about the way she is treated."

It was deliberately formal but I guessed the other woman was part of some activist group or other and would be well primed about the best ways to make trouble. The first thing to do is holler "Rape." That muddies up the water so you can get away with anything less than murder.

I spoke to the woman in the green skirt next, again making it deliberately formal. "Until your name is revealed, I am calling you Jane Doe." There was no answer so I rhymed off the caution and the new Charter of Rights routine.

She didn't answer. Instead she crossed her arms and stared at the floor as if waiting for the firing squad. Before I could ask her anything, the door behind me burst open and a man of about sixty came in with a woman ten or fifteen years younger right behind him.

"What's going on?" He spoke hoarsely and his face was veal-white, drained of blood. I wondered if he had a heart problem.

"Are you Mr. Carmichael?"

He didn't get a chance to answer. His wife did it for him. I'd heard the local gossip that said she was once an actress. Whatever the truth, she was in charge of this scene. "Look at this, for sweet Christ's sake," she shouted. "The only cop in this hole in the ground and he's standing around in here with two broads and an open rye bottle." She swung her expensively blonde-dyed head to me and demanded, "Why aren't you out looking for our daughter?"

"Our," I noticed. She must be the girl's stepmother, over-compensating for some hidden hatreds. "I'm conducting an investigation in here. If you want to shout, wait outside."

She opened her mouth to crank up the volume a little higher but her husband touched her arm. "Easy, Dot." It was the tone of voice I would have used with Sam. She stopped and looked at him, ready to spring into action again if he didn't make something happen at once. He came further into the room and sat down. His hand was shaking as he adjusted his chair.

"I'm Frank Carmichael. It's my daughter who vanished out there."

"Where have you been since?" It's a policeman's question —shocking, but fair. He waved it aside with a thin hand. It wouldn't be too long before his blonde wife was spending the insurance money, it seemed to me.

"I have angina. I'm afraid the shock was a bit much for me. My wife was administering my medication. We were in the cloakroom."

His wife had picked the bones out of my question and she suddenly roared again. "Are you suggesting we had something to do with what happened?"

I ignored her. "I'd prefer to talk to you somewhere private, but there isn't anywhere else." Mr. Carmichael nodded again and moved his jaw forward, rolling his nitro pill around under his tongue, I imagined. I filled him in on my theory that his daughter had gone voluntarily, which indicated to

22

me that this was some kind of practical joke she was playing and not a real abduction. His wife objected again.

"Are you accusing . . ."

"Please be quiet. You're upsetting your husband." I guess nobody had spoken to her that way since she left the chorus line. She almost bit her tongue.

"I am about to check the license number of the getaway vehicle. Give me one minute on the phone." I picked up the receiver, hoping that the snow hadn't brought the lines down.

I was lucky. A minute later I'd learned that the Toyota had been stolen late that afternoon from a ski resort south of here. If I'd been back to my office within the last couple of hours I would have seen the number on the teletype. I filled in the operator on what had happened and gave him a description of Nancy. I looked up at her mother. "What kind of coat did she have on?"

"She came here in a calf-length raccoon," she said.

"Check if it's still in the cloakroom, please."

She looked surprised at being asked to run errands and her husband said, "You can identify it, dear. These people couldn't."

It was quieter without her. I asked Carmichael, "Have you ever seen this woman before? Is she a friend of your daughter's?"

"If she is, she's a stranger to me." He was calmer now. The nitro had taken hold and the hoarseness was leaving his voice as the pain receded. I studied him as I spoke. He had the lean, city look of big business, but there was a toughness under it. He had been a soldier once, I'd learned that in local gossip. After the war he had come back and studied geology on a veteran's grant and had made a big strike in the late forties. From there he had gone into business in Toronto. His clothes told me that much, but his face looked rugged and there was a white crease in the hairline above his ear, the kind of gouge a bullet makes. He had come closer than this to death a long time ago.

"I think your daughter has set up this disappearance as a joke," I explained again. "Is she a high-spirited girl, would she do that kind of thing?" Meaning, is she a spoiled kid who enjoys making monkeys out of everybody.

He shrugged. "She's never done anything like that before."

I straightened up. "All right. Don't worry. I'm going to try to find out where she is. It will be difficult, so please be patient. In the meantime, I don't think she's in any danger." I was talking as much for the prisoner's benefit as for his, but she kept her face tilted down and if I'd hit the bull's eye she would never have let me know.

His wife came back into the room empty-handed. "Her coat's gone. That's a three-thousand-dollar raccoon. Somebody must have stolen it."

"She was probably wearing it when she left," I said.

This made her turn and flare at me. "What the hell are you talking about? What kind of a cop are you, anyway? You're nothing but a goddamn meter maid, working in this place."

Walter Puckrin chimed in now. "This man's the best policeman you've ever met. He took on three guys last summer, smart guys with guns, and killed the lot of them."

The prisoner looked up in terror. Nobody had given her my pedigree when they suggested Murphy's Harbour as the site of their caper. But it didn't fizz on Mrs. Carmichael.

"Well, get off your arse and kill somebody else, before our daughter freezes to death."

"You're not helping, Mrs. Carmichael. I'm sure your daughter is safe. I think this is some kind of prank. Just relax."

Her husband had taken her hand and was patting it. When she spoke again the respect was showing through her tone, like a fingertip through a torn glove.

"You really think that?"

I nodded. "Val, will you stay here with the prisoner? Walter, you get on with business. I've got an idea."

I went out into the hall. Sam was still waiting by the stage. I nodded, and he joined me as I went to the Legionnaire at the door, still sitting with his cash box and his beer, a fresh one.

"How many people bought tickets at the door?"

He pursed his lips thoughtfully. "None, I guess. All my sales is liquor and beer. Everybody had a ticket they bought ahead of time."

"Thanks. I need your box of stubs." I took the box and headed for the microphone. I knew what I had to do. It would be a painstaking job, but you don't get the chance to do any hundred-yard dashes at the start of an investigation. You have to find the facts. It's like picking fly dirt out of pepper.

I called on the women who had been in charge of selling tickets. They confirmed what I knew. The tickets were in three parts. The initial stub had a name and address written on it by the seller. It was put in the box for a draw for a pair of snowshoes. In addition, the guy at the door tore the remaining part of the ticket in half. They went in the box as well, so that people actually attending the dance had a double chance to win. It was typical small-town fussing, but it gave me a lead.

Moving quickly, I read out the numbers on the stubs in the box I'd picked up. As I did, the owner of the ticket went to one side of the hall. When I came to the ticket of a missing person I would know they had left with the girl.

I was halfway through the box before it happened. Ticket number 204. I called Val on the microphone and she checked the purse of the girl I'd arrested. She had no ticket of her own. "She ate it when you started calling numbers," Val told me, and the crowd laughed.

Behind me the wives of the Chamber of Commerce people were riffling through the names and addresses. They came up with number 204 and brought it to me.

It was made out to a Ms. Pankhurst and the address was a

place in Toronto. I thought back to my days as a Toronto policeman and realized that it was the address of one of the police stations. I had been outsmarted by the buyer.

"Did you sell this ticket yourself?"

The woman shook her head. "No, that's not my writing, Chief. Let me think. I did give out a couple to other people to sell. Lee Chong at the restaurant got a book. So did Fred Wales at the Muskellunge Motel."

We both stared at the writing, which was square and neat. The name of the street in Toronto had been misspelled.

"That's Fred Wales," I guessed, and she agreed. "Must be. I can't hardly read Lee's writing, so this can't be his."

We were talking away from the microphone, me crouching at the side of the stage looking down at her. She was fiftyish and serious. "Don't tell a soul about this. It's important," I told her.

She nodded. "If you say, Chief." She would help me, for now. Tomorrow this would be her war story and she would bore the Ladies' Aid with it from here on.

I collected Val Summers from Puckrin's office, leaving Sam on guard over the girl. Walter was happy to lend me his Blazer again. The door to his office was open, and the dancers were staring in as they passed, envying him his share of the limelight. He had built a deep, dark drink and was ready to sit there all evening if he had to, counting cash and trying to get Jane Doe to say something.

The girl was getting restless. She had expected more interest than this. For her few moments she had been a star and she had liked it. Now she was a nobody and it rankled. I was glad to see it. She would be talkative next time I questioned her, anxious to prove how important she had been in the plan. For now I left her in Sam's care.

The snow hit us like a club when we left the hall. Already four inches had come down, and it had drifted a yard deep in the lee of the pines along the side of the road to the highway, thumping under my tires, obscuring even the marks I had

26

made a few minutes earlier. Driving was difficult. The road-bed was anybody's guess. Twice in the mile to the highway I slipped off the pavement onto the shoulder, but the four-wheel drive dug in and hung on, holding us safe.

"The motel's just north of the corner. There's a chance they've been dumb enough to head right back there. If they have, we've got them. If they haven't—well, at least we'll get a description, maybe even a license number from Fred Wales. They must have bought the tickets there, maybe tonight."

"If all they want is publicity for this C.L.A.W. outfit, maybe they'll head there and sit tight," Val said. Her voice was the only warmth in the night and her perfume was a promise of springtime.

I had put our date out of my mind. For now I was a police-man earning the small amount of pay I got by solving the biggest problem to hit Murphy's Harbour in six months. Later, when the hassle was over, I looked forward to my weekend with Val. I reached out and squeezed her knee. She covered my hand with hers and we drove out to the highway in comfortable silence.

The drift at the road junction was deeper now, but Walter's vehicle made it on the second try and I headed north, the way the getaway car had been pointing. I was a little angry with myself for not pushing on earlier in hot pursuit. But I'd had nothing to go on then—any parked car at roadside would have made me stop to investigate. I would have gotten nowhere. Now I was feeling confident again.

We reached the Muskellunge Motel and pulled in. It's the typical northern Ontario stop-over, a row of cabins with the office-cum-coffee-shop-cum-living quarters for the owner at one end. I parked outside the coffee shop and sent Val inside to drum up Fred Wales while I took a quick walk along the line of cabins. There were cars parked in front of most of them, but the one I wanted was outside number six. It was a big Ford station wagon and the hood was still warm enough that the new snow was melting where it fell, leaving only

27

the outline of the bracing members under the hood. I guessed it had been in its place for about half an hour. The timing was right.

There were lights on in the cabin but I backed away without knocking. If the kidnappers were less dumb than they looked at this moment, they would have parked in front of the wrong cabin, giving themselves time to escape when the big slow copper came banging on someone else's door. I would check first.

Fred Wales was pouring coffee for Val, excited at the presence of a good-looking woman on a night when only truck drivers would normally come in. He's a tall thin Englishman who's been here since the war but has never lost his accent. He thinks his slang makes him sound North American. Most of it comes from late movies.

"Hi," he said. "Long time no see."

"Official business, Fred." I sat down and sipped my coffee, but kept my hat on and my parka zipped so he would know this was not a social call. "What can you tell me about the party in number six?"

"Hang on, I'll check." He beamed at Val again and went out through the back door. Val grinned at me. I winked back.

"Here it is." He returned with a sheaf of cards in his hand. "A woman, Ms. Ann Gree."

I snorted. "Not trying very hard to fool us, are they?"

Val laughed. "Ann Gree, with a Ms. She's sure teed off with you male chauvs, that's certain."

I took the card from Wales. It was filled out in a clear, literate hand, a schoolteacher's script.

"Can I see the others, Fred? I'm looking for women on their own, pairs of girls, maybe even three together."

Wales handed over the cards and rubbed his chin. "No, everybody else was couples, except for one trucker and a guy, said he was on his own."

28

One of the cards read: George Nighswander. The address was the one I'd seen on Nighswander's license at the Tavern. "You sure he was alone? I think he's gay."

Wales shrugged. "I don't go out to check. The window was snowed up at the office. He said he was alone." He was losing interest in us. Most likely *Casablanca* was on TV from Parry Sound. He was hoping we would clear out and leave him alone to get on with being snowed in.

"When I saw him he had a couple of other guys with him, looked light."

"I didn't see anybody," Wales said patiently. "An' what the eye don't see, the heart don't grieve over."

"Thanks anyway. One last thing. When did you sell your book of tickets for the dance?"

"Tickets? Why?"

"Just checking. Can you remember?"

He rubbed his chin with one finger, making a rasping sound I could hear above the Muzak. "Last Saturday. A woman came in an' bought all ten. Just like that."

"Thanks." I wondered if we had ten people working against us tonight. "I'll just go call on Ms. Gree."

Wales was alarmed. "Hey, go easy, Chief. There's no law against her giving a phony name."

There is, but it's never enforced. I pulled down the flaps around my hat. It looks silly, but it saves your ears from frostbite and that's not silly. "Don't worry. I don't care about any Smiths you get in here, just her."

That bothered him. His accent lost thirty years and became bitingly British. "I run a respectable place."

"I know. They get their share of Smiths in the Royal York in Toronto. But this girl could be important."

Val was standing, buttoning her coat. "She could be involved in a kidnapping at the Legion," she offered, and Wales gasped.

He gave us the key with no more argument and we walked

to cabin six. We stood there perhaps thirty seconds, listening hard, but could make out nothing over the rush of the wind and the white-sound hiss of the snow against our collars and faces.

Finally I turned to Val and shrugged, then knocked at the door. There was no answer and I waited another twenty seconds, taking a few steps to each side of the cabin, making sure no one was coming out of the sides or the back.

I opened the door and a gust of warm air enveloped me. I took one sniff and told Val, "Wait by the door, something's wrong." She didn't understand me but did as I said anyway. I stuck my right hand deep in my parka pocket, holding my gun ready for trouble.

The bedroom was empty. The bed was rumpled as if someone had sat on it. It looked as if the cabin was empty but I knew better. The place smelled of death.

I pulled my gun and slammed the bathroom door open with a kick, trying to shock whoever was hiding there.

It was too late. The girl who was hanging from the shower rail had been dead for at least fifteen minutes.

5

The face was bloated and inhuman, but I could tell that the body was not Nancy Carmichael's. This was another girl, as close to thirty as she was ever going to get. She was naked and her sphincter had failed her. I knew she was dead but I'm not a doctor, not qualified to make judgments like that. I took out my clasp knife and cut her down. I spent a fruitless couple of minutes breathing into her lungs and pounding her chest but I was too late. Val came in on tiptoe, frightened, saw the corpse, and vomited into the bathtub. "Don't touch anything," I told her. She tore some tissues from the container, not touching the metal, and wiped her mouth.

"Go back to the office and wait. Watch to make sure nobody leaves. If they do, check their car number and come and tell me right away. Can you do that? Please?"

She nodded and left. I stood up, leaving the girl lying face up on the floor, my eyes checking everything in the room. Nothing was disturbed. The pile of towels was untouched, the paper flag was across the toilet seat, there were no signs of any struggle. It could have meant that she had rented the room and simply walked in and committed suicide. But I didn't think so.

I bent and examined the mark on the throat. It was as I had guessed. There were two marks. One had been made by something broader than the thin cord of pantyhose used as a ligament for the hanging. To my eye it seemed as if the neck had been crushed by a blow, possibly a classic karate chop. Then, before the body was completely past the point of no return, it had been hung from the shower rail. I was dealing with a murder.

There was nothing else constructive to do in the bathroom. Later, when I had come to the end of the immediate things—the single-handed chasing I would have to do until I found the Carmichael kid—I would come back and spend the necessary hours here. For now I stepped back, checking visually that there were no obvious footprints on the tile.

The bedroom yielded more. Nothing tangible, but I have a jungle-fighter's nose. It had saved my life in Nam. I'd picked up the ammonia smell of sweat on a trail before I turned what would have been my last corner into the ambush. I had hosed down the jungle and killed the man who was waiting to kill me.

Now I was picking up a different scent. It was amplified by the overheated air of the cabin, reaching me even over the human smells from the dead girl in the bathroom and acidity of Val's vomit. It was perfume, the same scent I had noticed in the Toyota. I put my gloves on and opened the dead girl's purse. There was a different perfume inside— "Charlie," a light, almost neuter fragrance, not like the heaviness of the Carmichael girl's performing scent.

There was nothing in the purse to identify the body. No credit cards, no license. I checked the suitcase, there was nothing, not even a monogram on the blouses to indicate who the dead girl was. I took a final look under the bed, finding nothing, then went out, locking the cabin behind me.

In passing I checked the license plates on the station wagon, noting the number. Then I ran to the coffee shop.

Val was sitting with a glass of something dark, rum by the

look of it. Fred Wales was standing over her, hands raised as if caught in a strobe light doing some frantic dance. He turned to me when I came in. "Christ, Chief, what's happening?"

"Looks like a homicide, Fred. Give me all the other keys to that cabin and let me use your phone."

I dialed the Ontario Provincial Police detachment to report the murder. The operator told me that the station wagon had also been stolen that morning, from a ski resort close to Orillia. I gave him a description of Nighswander and his address—wanted for questioning—and hung up. Wales brought me all the keys for cabin six and a cup of coffee. I sat and sipped, not talking, trying to work out what to do next. The obvious thing would be to go over the murder scene minutely. That's what any regular department would do because any regular department has men to spare for jobs like that. I don't. If there's a choice between thinking work and hot pursuit, I have to take the pursuit.

I was wondering if the dead girl had been intended as a sacrifice, a gambit to put me off the chase. Maybe she had also been a prospect for dropping out of C.L.A.W. and filling me in with some details. Now she would tell me nothing. But, I resolved, she wouldn't hold me back, either. I would keep on chasing Nancy Carmichael any way I could, tugging at all the leads until they had unraveled or led me to her. This was a bad night for police work, but it was also a bad night for people planning a getaway. If someone had taken the girl away by car, they might be stuck in a ditch right now waiting for a policeman to come by. There was nothing moving but fools, criminals, and coppers.

I left Val finishing her rum and went from door to door along the row of cabins. In four of them, including the truck driver's, I found couples, two of them obvious mismatches, worried that a jealous husband had sent me to check on them. None of them had seen anything. None of them was suspicious. I opened the cabin Nighswander had

33

rented and in it found my only clue. Beside the bed, looking as if it had been dropped in a hurry, lay the top of a swimsuit similar to the one the Carmichael girl had worn at the pageant. It was fragrant with the same perfume.

I phoned the police in Toronto and asked them to stake out Nighswander's home. I also called the doctor in Murphy's Harbour but he wasn't home. Probably he was at the dance. He must have been wearing one of the skinny girl's masks, and after the disappearance, when people took off their masks, I hadn't noticed him. I would have to wait until morning for his assistance at the murder scene.

It still felt wrong. It was all too obvious. If Nighswander had been intending to kill the girl he wouldn't have gotten into that fight earlier, where everyone could see him. And was it him, anyway? I could sense a connection but there was nothing to match him up with the dead girl, only with the one who had disappeared. I sat on the edge of his bed and thought about it for a minute or two but could see nothing brilliant to do. The only thing I knew was that the puzzle was in pieces and the pieces were scattering themselves wider all the time.

I took Val from the coffee shop and drove back to the Legion Hall as fast as I dared on the snowed-in road. It was beginning to get frightening. The road was hidden under eight or ten inches of new snow, up to four feet in the drifts, and my eyes were dazzled with the flakes spiraling down my headlights to crackle against the windshield. Val said nothing. I glanced at her once or twice but she was staring ahead, her lips moving. She might have been praying.

At the Legion, things were getting boisterous. Everyone was committed to staying all night and they were all drinking more than they would have done normally. It was hot and noisy and lively, and the missing girl was a joke. I was glad I'd stayed cool about it. They all thought they were in on a prank. It was easier that way.

34

People caught at me and tried to talk as I went through to the office where Puckrin was still sitting with his bottle. Val was right behind me.

Walter Puckrin was feeling good. The rye and ginger were working on him and he was enjoying the limelight. "Talkative little devil," he told me jovially. " 'Part from telling me to go screw myself, she hasn't said boo."

"Thanks, Walter. It's time to tuck her in for the night." I touched the seated woman on the shoulder. "On your feet, please, I'm taking you to the station."

She looked up at me, not moving, debating what her civil-disobedience friends would have recommended. She decided to ignore me, so I turned away and stooped to pat Sam and give him a quiet little hiss, one of his signals to give tongue. He bounced to his feet and barked at her, his big head almost at face level. She shrieked and stood up. I told Sam "Easy," and he fell silent. The woman came with us then, walking quietly between Val and me to the cloakroom for her coat and to the door. I told the Legionnaire: "Anybody wants to leave, tell them I said not to. It's a killer out there."

He was working on another Export. It must have been his eighth, and he waved a tipsy hand. "No sweat, Chief, I'll keep the bastards here."

I put the girl in the back seat of the Blazer. Val sat next to her and I walked around, swooping off the snow that had collected on the vehicle while I was inside. When I got behind the wheel with Sam in the passenger seat, I started up and turned to the prisoner. "Your friend at the highway was murdered." She said nothing, although I could see her mouth working. Then I gave her the rest of it. It was brutal but I had to crack her pose some way. I needed information and quickly. "Somebody hit her in the throat, then hung her from the shower rail."

She screamed, low and anguished, then covered her face

35

and sobbed. Val put one hand on her shoulder but said nothing. I was glad she was there.

The station was in darkness. I don't bother lighting it at night, especially in winter. I don't live there. I have a house on the north edge of town. The station stays closed up except when I'm inside. The best way to reach the department is to phone. The operator will call on the radio in the scout car if we have an emergency. Only tonight the scout car was sitting on flat tires in front of the Legion.

Snow had drifted seven feet deep against the side door where I normally admit prisoners, so I parked in front and went in the way citizens come in under their own steam. I put the lights on and they buzzed and flickered a moment or two. The room was cool—I keep the thermostat down low. I lifted the flap in the counter and led the women through to the back.

There isn't much to see in the station. The front office has a couple of desks and an old manual typewriter, a stationery cupboard and file cabinets, a gun rack with rifle and shotgun, and the teletype machine. That's it. A few months previously, on a slow fall day, I had painted the walls. I thought yellow would be a change from the standard dull green. Under the blue-green of the lights it just looked bilious.

The woman was still crying. I let her sob. Maybe it would lubricate her tongue, and she would give me something more than her number, rank, and name. If she didn't, I was all out of things to do to trace Nancy Carmichael.

The back of the station is a narrow hallway. On one side is a white wall—I had, thank God, run out of yellow by then —with a table and chair. On the other side are our cells, both of them empty.

I sat the girl in the chair and picked up the clipboard that lay on the table. The girl went on sobbing helplessly and I said to Val, "Would you get the young lady some water and a Kleenex, please?"

The girl took the enamel mug as if it were a chalice, holding it in both hands, sipping between sobs. I crouched down until I was at her eye level. "I'm sorry about your friend. She looked as if she was an attractive and intelligent young woman."

"She was," the girl said, and sobbed quickly one last time. She repeated, "She was."

"Now you know she's dead, you must understand that whoever got you into this affair is not playing games. They're wicked people."

Wicked was the right word. It made everything sound like a fairy story. It might even make me a knight on a white horse. The girl looked at me, then glanced away. "I didn't think anything bad would happen."

"It happened," Val said. "She's dead." Her voice was harsh, and I realized it was the first time she had spoken since leaving the motel. She was badly shaken.

"What's her name?" I asked the girl.

She looked at me honestly. "I don't know. There were four of us. What did she look like?"

I described the girl to her but she shook her head.

"You were part of the same organization. You must know her."

"I do. But not her name. Not her real name, anyway."

"Were you working under some kind of security?"

She nodded almost eagerly. She wanted me to know. "It was very tight. All we used were first names, and I don't think they were all real."

It didn't look as if she was going to be much help but she was all I had. I pushed a little harder. "What names did you use in your group?"

The girl sniffed and wiped her eyes on her sleeve. She looked as frail and vulnerable as a ten-year-old. "She called herself Katie. Then there were two others, Rachael and Freddie. And me, of course."

"Freddie, was that a man?" Men joined feminist groups,

supported them, anyway. I'd seen them in the parades when I was a young policeman just back from Viet Nam and angry at all the protesters.

"No." The girl was sure of that. "She called herself Freddie because she wanted to be like a man. But she wasn't —she was a girl, my age, about."

"Did this Katie come up here with the rest of you, or did she come with someone else?"

The girl looked at me levelly, telling the truth without reservation. "She came with a guy. She called him her boy-friend, but I don't think there was anything between them."

"Did you hear his name? Did you ever meet him?"

She shook her head. A strand of her mousy hair had come undone, and it wagged in front of her forehead like an antenna. "I never met him. She wouldn't introduce him."

"Did she give you any idea of what he looked like? Did she tell you he was dark, fair, tall, short?"

She pursed her lips and shook her head. I thought for a moment she would not speak, but she was thinking. Finally she said, "She called him a rough diamond once. Said we shouldn't judge by appearances when we met him."

Rough diamond! Scratch Nighswander. You could put him in dungarees and hand him a shovel and he would still come out a smoothie. If he hadn't killed this Katie, who had? And why?

I backed away from that line of questioning and tried for more background. It might loosen up something in her memory or lead me to the rest of the gang. "How did you meet up with the others?"

This was more personal than she liked. She pulled a handkerchief from her sleeve and began folding it into tiny tucks. "I was approached."

"Who by?"

"I don't know her name. She came up to me in court, afterward, and asked me if I'd be interested in joining a group that would make men sorry for the way they abused us."

That raised a lot of questions that I stored in my head. What was she doing in court, for one thing. And how did the woman who approached her know that this particular skinny girl was anti-men? But that could all wait for the brandy and cigars after we'd consumed the worthwhile evidence, if she had any to give me.

"Could you tell me about the woman who came up to you—her name, what she looked like, what she said to you, anything you can remember?" I asked it softly and she did not answer at once, just kept on folding the handkerchief until I reminded her, "A member of your group has been killed. If I can find the person at the center of the group, I can let her know. She can warn the others to be on their guard."

Now she looked up, keeping her hands busy, pitty-patting the folded handkerchief. "Is that what you'd do, really?"

"Straight up." In the mood of this interrogation I sketched a cross over my heart with my right hand. It worked. Over the next five minutes she gave me all the information she had.

She had been the victim of an attempted rape. She had accepted a ride home from some guy she met at a party. He had been acquitted because the judge thought she should have shown better judgment than to go off with a stranger. As she was leaving the court, humiliated, while the accused was shaking hands with his friends, she had been approached by a woman in her fifties. They had gone for coffee together. My prisoner had been ashamed and depressed and the woman had been sympathetic. The other woman had told her that there was a new group being formed to heighten the awareness of men to the humiliation of women.

I asked her to repeat that part and she gave it back to me word for word. Obviously I had some pop psychology coming at me from this mysterious, murderous grandmother.

The woman had not given a full name. "You call me Margaret," was all she gave away. She had invited the girl to a meeting, which was held a week later in a motel room on the edge of Toronto. The girl had gone and met three other women of about her own age, all of them angry over some feminist cause. One had been a battered wife. One had been harassed by an employer with more hands than sense. The other one had no specific beef but it seemed to my prisoner that she was angry at all men.

"She struck you as lesbian?"

"I'm not saying that. She seemed angry, as I said—more than the rest of us, and we all had some good cause for anger." Between them they had hatched up the plot to abduct Nancy and gain publicity for their cause. She insisted that Nancy had been a party to the idea. They would not have forced her, they were all too anxious to protect one another's rights as women, she told me.

It rang true. If the kidnapping had been carried out by force, it would have taken at least two people to drag Nancy to the waiting car. As it was she had gone cleanly—her footprints had told me that. This girl confirmed it.

When it came to her own part in the affair, she was more reticent. I found out at last that she had been told to strip while the crowd was watching the beauty parade and to jump out as soon as the lights came on again after Nancy's disappearance. But she had been too timid and had spent ten minutes psyching herself up for the exposure.

I nodded and made tut-tut noises, and then threw her the hard question. "One girl is dead and Nancy is gone. Do you still think it's a joke?"

It scared her, but she had no information. She had carried out her orders and was waiting for her group leader to pat her on the head and tell her she had done well. Only there was a corpse in the picture now and it wasn't a prank any more. All she could do was to weep and insist that she had

40

no idea where Nancy had gone. The plan had been for her to stay at the motel until morning, when she would emerge and make her speech about male chauvinism while the whole of the beauty contest judging panel hung its head in shame. It was all very bloody smug. And it was also a crock. There was more to this operation than the phony kidnapping. It looked to me as if somebody wanted to get their hands on the girl, perhaps for ransom, and had set up this spurious group to do the dirty work and act as a smoke screen. I was growing certain that professionals had removed the girl from the removers while the removers all struck their little poses.

Val found coffee and made a full pot. We all had a cup while I talked the girl through her story again. She came up with the dots for a couple of "i"s and the crosses for the "t"s, but nothing new. I decided to ring the motel where the meeting had taken place, on the outside chance that Fred might remember this Margaret and that she had used her real name to register for the room. After that, I was stumped. Nancy Carmichael could be fifty miles south of here by now, still not realizing that she was in danger. I had no way of letting her know.

The phone ring was a relief. I picked it up at once. That's my arrangement with the woman who answers the extension for me while I'm away. I take it when I'm at home or after ten o'clock at night.

"Police Department."

"Reid. Come right away. They've been here. They took all my film. All my goddamn film. Everything." Carl Simmonds was almost soprano in his anger. I told him to wait there and hung up.

Val looked up, waiting instructions. I said, "I want you to stay and make sure our visitor doesn't come to any harm. I have to go to see the photographer."

"Does he have something for you—a clue?"

"Yes," I lied. "Meantime, make yourself comfortable. There's blankets under the counter if you need them. Bunk down in the spare cell and snooze. I'll leave Sam minding the store."

Two minutes later they were both in cells, one locked, one unlocked, and I was on the station skidoo heading for Carl's cottage. It had taken me most of the two minutes to get out of the garage past the snowdrift. I'd ended up trampling it solid at one end so it would bear the weight of the machine. As a result, I was soaked with perspiration but cooling in the relentless wind, still flushing snow at me as if it would never end.

I have never worked out why city people buy snowmobiles and ride them for fun. Up here they're a tool, a vehicle that does the work of a dog team, without the fighting. But they're no fun to ride, especially on a night like this one.

By the time I got to Carl's place I could feel the beginnings of frostbite. There was almost no sensation in my cheeks and nose. I stood and pounded on his front door and pounded my frozen face with alternate hands until he opened up for me. I wished he would hurry. There were skidoo tracks on the road but I had no idea which way to follow them, and no idea who to look for if the tracks led to a crowd like there was at the Lakeside or the Legion. I needed some quick details from Carl and I could go after whoever had taken his film.

I had never been in Carl's house before but had expected taste and elegance. Yesterday, things probably were that way. Tomorrow for sure, but tonight there was a welter of furniture, magazines, books, pictures, all tossed anyhow into the center of the living room. Carl was still wearing the clothes he'd had on at the Legion Hall, but the pockets in the jacket had been cut away raggedly.

He said nothing to me as I entered, but stood there for me to check the damage and whistle.

"Were they looking for the photographs you took at the Ball?"

"That's what they said." He tossed his head to throw back his long blonde hair and waved his hands despairingly. "For a couple of lousy negatives they did this."

I moved further into the room, stepping over the rubble, stooping to pick up a book. I closed it, noting automatically the title *Out of Africa*. "How many were there?"

"Three of them, all wearing blue skidoo suits, one-piece jobs like the kind they sell in Canadian Tire. They all had red ski masks over their faces."

"All dressed identically?"

He nodded. "And very bloody tacky they looked, too."

"Were they men, women, how tall, how heavy? I need anything you noticed, I want a handle on this thing."

He was bending down to pick up an ebony carving that must have been some kind of fertility symbol. He noticed me watching him and went a little red, dropping the statue and straightening up, wiping his palms on his thighs. "Okay. I'm wasting time. Let me get a drink and I'll sit and concentrate."

I didn't need a drink, but I wanted his concentration so I said nothing. He set a small sideboard back on its legs. It looked as if it cost as much as my house. He opened the front and swore once as liquor from a smashed bottle ran out onto his rug, a sand-colored Moslem carpet of some kind. He pulled out a bottle of Hennessy and two glasses, one of them snapped off at the stem. He poured about four ounces into each and handed the complete one to me. I nodded thanks and took it. I needed his memory. He was a photographer, he used his eyes better than most people.

"What happened was I was working in the darkroom when they came in. The door at the side was locked, they smashed a pane of glass and let themselves in that way." He took a sip of his cognac and sat down, cross-legged among

43

the ruined books and paintings. "I came out of the dark-room when I heard the noise."

Now he straightened up suddenly, importantly, and walked to the back entrance to the room. "I was standing here and I said, 'What the hell is going on?' Something like that. Then the leader said. 'Give us the negatives, faggot.' "

"The leader?" I prodded quickly.

He shrugged. "Seemed to be. He was the only one to speak the whole time they were here. The others did as he told them. He had the authority, I suppose you'd say."

"You're sure it was a man?"

He cocked his head toward me, surprised. "Of course, why?"

I gave him a little of the detail about C.L.A.W. that the prisoner had told me. "It's some kind of feminist movement. There may be men in it but they don't figure prominently so far."

He sipped his cognac, then stood swirling it in the broken-stemmed glass. From his gesture this might have been an ordinary night and he would have been listening to Mozart on his stereo and having a nightcap in comfort. I felt sorry for him, but I was even more sorry for the girl at the motel and beginning to feel sorry for the Carmichael kid.

"Let me replay this, if you don't mind," he said at last. I waved one hand in silence and he went out, scrunching over the debris, to the back door of his summer kitchen. He paused as he came back, balancing his glass on top of a plant pot that was still standing in the window.

Now he advanced to the center of the room, stood still for a moment, backed off, advanced again, knelt down to his right side, covering his head with his left hand, then stood up.

"The man was in front. He was close to your height, maybe five-eleven, well built. He was right-handed." He paused and thought for a moment. "He was the one who

44

hit me and then showed the others how to shake the place down like this. He's the sonofabitch I hope you catch."

"What color were his eyes?" I asked quietly.

"Brown," Carl said without hesitation. "So were the eyes of the second person—slim hips, might have been a woman or a small man. I couldn't tell, he or she didn't move around much." He hissed, suddenly angry. "If he–she had moved much I would have known. You can always tell if it's a man by the articulation of the legs. Queens don't fool anybody."

"What about the third one? What color eyes, any hair showing, what?"

Carl put his hand to his chin, then clasped the other hand across his chest to lock the elbow. It was the move Jack Benny used to make on TV when the world was younger and warmer and things other than pain and humiliation were worth a laugh.

"Undoubtedly a woman," he decided. "Not much in the boobies department, rather heavier in the hips, about five-four, perhaps one-thirty." He stopped for so long I was about to ask him another question before he said, "And she had brown eyes with seven gold flecks in the left pupil."

"You're kidding!" I almost laughed. To stand in the wreckage of your home and take notice of that kind of detail called for a toughness of spirit most people don't have.

"Absolutely true," he said, throwing up his hands. "I know you're going to catch her and when you do, I'll identify her for you."

"So. Okay. What exactly happened after he hit you?" I was scribbling the descriptions in my book as I talked and he paused a moment to let me catch up.

"They looked for the negatives of the film I had shot at the Ball. They got them right away, I hadn't even had time to print them up. Then, just to be sure, I guess, they did all this."

45

"Was that the only reason, do you think?" It was a guess, but this was turning into an unusual case. I wondered if one of the C.L.A.W. people had been a closet gay, resentful about his leanings, carrying on the ancient sport of fagbashing.

Carl went back to his cognac and took a solid bite out of it. "I think the man was enjoying himself," he said simply.

"I'll try to get them all," I promised. "I saw skidoo tracks outside, just point which way they went and I'll follow."

He came to the door with me as I zipped up my parka and pulled down the flaps on my fur hat. It was savagely cold at his door but he stood there in his light jacket without shivering as he pointed out the direction they had taken. I admire that little guy. As I got on the machine he called out, "They went thataway!" and laughed.

I laughed and started my skidoo. I didn't need to be an Australian bushman to follow the trail. Once he had told me which way was coming and which one going, I followed the overlapping belt tracks at close to thirty miles an hour. It seemed to me there were only two tracks. One person must have been riding pillion. On the machine it was almost calm as I ran with the wind at my back. The tracks were still crisp and fresh, only beginning now to drift in.

Within two hundred yards they left the roadway and turned up over the rocks that loomed bare red in the headlights, swept clear of snow by the relentless wind. I followed up through the trees and onto an old logging trail that had been recleared that fall for snowmobiling. It was all part of the Reeve's plan for winter fun and games. He hadn't counted on its being used as a getaway road. But maybe the escapers hadn't reckoned on my following them, so I wound up the throttle and pushed on as fast as I could in the flat footprint of the machine ahead. The track led to a small open shelter in a clearing. It's not fancy—three walls and a roof with a stone fireplace. It's not worth vandalizing, and it's stood up for a few years now of snowmobiler rendezvous. The tracks turned into the front of it and I pulled in just behind, where they had obviously stopped. There was a welter of footprints and unmistakable evidence that a man had relieved himself, outside the shelter, out of sight. That meant Carl was right. At least one of the party was a man.

I checked the ground and decided that the two machines had met up with a third. It was hard to examine the footprints in the snow with a flashlight, but it seemed that two other people had been waiting here. That meant I had five of them to worry about. I flashed the light around the shelter, but whoever it was had not whiled away the time carving their initials or leaving their wallets, so I was no further ahead. There was nothing to do but get back on my machine and follow the triple track further on down another branch of the trail.

I could tell from a sudden dip that I must be nearing the lake, but was still surprised to burst suddenly out of the trees through one long snowdrift which had fortunately been beaten down enough by the people ahead that my machine didn't flounder. I gasped with cold as a long-bow wave of snow flung itself back over me, and I craned up tall to see over the windshield. The machine was not new and the windshield was scratched. With the loose snow on it, I couldn't see through. And now I needed to. The surface of the lake was frozen a foot thick, but on top of the ice the old snow had thawed in our bright January sunshine and refrozen until it was mirror slick. There were clear patches like this one all over the lake. Where the snow had clung it would be easy to follow the skidoo tracks, but here with new snow blowing, dry as sand over the smooth surface, I had to count on luck.

I slowed my speed to just above walking pace, finding the beam of my light picking up dimples on the surface where falling snow had been crimped under the belts of the ma-

47

chines ahead and had stood long enough to sculpt its own tiny drifts. As I went on, my head stuck out to the side of the windshield, I gradually picked up the pace to perhaps half the speed the others would be making, moving surely to a destination somewhere on the lake. I had worked out that much. They had no other reason for heading north as they were doing, away from the highway. And that meant I was within six or seven miles of them, perhaps of the missing girl. I might even wrap up this case and make it home by midnight.

And so I drove on, warmed by my own cleverness behind my single cone of light that picked up a million driven sparks of snow and the tiny crusted remains of a track in front of me.

At the very limit of my vision I saw something dark and square edged, low to the ice. I slowed a fraction before the geometry made sense. It was an ice-fishing hut out over the deep shoals in mid-channel where the big pickerel spend their winter. There is a village of them out there, from late December until March, when I would start handing out warnings to bring them in before the breakup.

A second hut came in view, and then a third, and then something so startling I let go of the handles of the machine to rub my eyes. The machine slowed to a stop on its dead-man's throttle and I started out again slowly, not sure what I had seen. It was tall and white, flashing even whiter than the merciless snow. I wondered if it was an albino deer, and then my headlight caught it again and I drove up as fast as I could to the running woman, naked as the day she was born, screaming in a long formless wail.

6

I slammed the machine to a stop alongside her but she turned away, leaping over the surface as if the ice were hot instead of killing cold. Bundled up as I was in a parka and skidoo boots over my regular indoor uniform, I could not move fast and it took me thirty yards to catch up with her. I had to tackle her and drag her down like a rugby player. She screamed and fought, but I tore my parka off and bundled it around her and suddenly she stopped struggling and crouched there, whimpering like a child.

I picked her up, clear of the frozen surface. She pulled up her legs, trying to snuggle them out of the wind inside my short parka as I struggled to the skidoo and sat her in front of me behind the windshield. "Sit still," I ordered over the noise of the wind and the ticking motor.

I got on behind her, pulling her against me with my left hand as I opened the throttle, searching ahead for the closest fishing hut. I knew she would never make it to the mainland without freezing, probably losing both feet to frostbite. I had to get her under cover where it was warm.

I found a hut and stopped. "Stay put," I shouted, and went to the door. It was locked on a flimsy hasp, but I kicked it once and it opened. I went back for the woman, picking her up and carrying her into the hut. Her teeth were chattering like typewriter keys and she was shuddering so hard she shook in my arms. I knelt at the door and pushed her in. Then I pulled out my flashlight and followed her. It was the standard local hut, made from sheets of plywood lying on their sides, four feet apart. The roof was made of two more sheets and the ends were the same, cut to shape with a door one end, a window the other. Inside was a hole in the ice, bathtub sized, a bare wooden bench eighteen inches wide, and a tiny homemade stove about the size of one of the tins of cookies came in when I was a kid. I helped her onto the seat and bent to the stove. There was a pile of wood chips beside it. I pulled my gloves off and took out my pocket knife. Working as quickly as I could I split one chip into slivers, then reached in my pocket for my notebook and ripped out a handful of pages. I crumpled them and put them in the stove, then the slivers on top. I always carry emergency matches in a waterproof tobacco can and I took it out and lit the fire. Within thirty seconds it had taken hold and I fed in more wood, slowly at first, then half filling the stove. The wind outside sucked the flames up around the raw wood and in another minute the hut was beginning to warm.

I turned then, still crouching, and looked at the girl. In the beam of my flashlight her face looked blue with cold. She blinked against the light and I could see that her eyes were gray. She had not been at the shivaree at Carl's house. "Will that bench move?" I asked her. I tugged at it, but it had frozen into the ice surface. The girl said nothing, just shivered, although her teeth had stopped chattering. I said, "Stretch your feet out to the stove. I'll get more wood from the other huts."

I ran across to the nearest hut, feeling the chill knife through my summer tunic as if it was a mosquito net. The hut was locked but I kicked it in and went inside. There was a pile of wood chips and, even more important, an empty beer can. I picked it up, along with the wood, and ran back to the first hut.

The girl was reviving. She had slipped her arms into the sleeves of my parka and was sitting with hands and feet stretched out straight toward the stove. I dropped the wood and drew my stick to break through the new ice in the fishing hole. It gave easily, only an inch or so thick, and I filled the beer can with water and set it on the stove. It hissed as spilled water boiled instantly on the hot metal. "I'll have a hot drink for you in a minute," I told her. "Now, why don't you tell me who you are and how the hell you got out here in the nude?"

The question broke her down. She began to weep helplessly, sobbing so hard it made her outstretched arms jerk convulsively. She was in shock and I knew that talking to her would do no good. Instead I said, "Feel in the top left-hand pocket of the parka." I had to repeat it but then she came to and did as I asked. Inside she found a Cadbury's Thick bar, wrapped in aluminum foil. It's the other half of my emergency gear. I never go outdoors in winter without knife, matches, and candy. That's enough to keep you alive indefinitely if you don't panic. The feel of the candy stopped her tears. She slowed to a snuffle and began to unwrap it, crushing the paper in her hand neatly and dropping it on top of the firewood. Then she bit into the chocolate with a survivor's fury, twice, three times, until her mouth was so full she could hardly chew.

I let her finish the bar, then hoisted the beer can off the stove. It was hot to the touch, and she made a little hurt sound as I gave it to her but drank obediently until it was all gone. I took the can off her, refilled it, and set it back on the stove. Already, the hut was warm enough for me to be comfortable in my summer clothes. Within minutes it would be too hot. If I were fishing here I would have to take off my jacket. The girl was warm enough to talk now.

"Okay. You're thawed out now. Tell me what happened."

She hesitated for a moment. I had put my flashlight away and the only light in the hut was the flicker of flames through a crack in the stove. Her face was a ripple of shadows that shattered suddenly as she began to talk, the words tumbling urgently out on top of one another. "It was awful. They made me undress. I said 'No.' I thought they were kidding, you know. I mean, it was terrible, but he hit me and they took my clothes off and drove away and left me. I was trying to catch up with them but they wouldn't stop."

"Who are *they*?"

I took my light out again and flicked it over her face. There were no bruises apparent, but her face was still pinched with cold. It would have been hard to read any marks more subtle than a black eye. I could see that she was pretty, prettier than the corpse in cabin six had been. This one could be a model. I wondered where she fit into the crazy puzzle.

"I was riding behind Rachael. I didn't know the others. We had never met them."

"Rachael who?" Rachael had been one of the other women my prisoner had mentioned.

"I don't know her last name. We just used first names."

"You were a part of the C.L.A.W.? You and Rachael and Katie?"

She nodded eagerly. "That's right, and Billie. Did she tell you about C.L.A.W.? Or was it Katie? She always did have trouble keeping security, Katie did."

"Katie is dead." My light was on her face and I saw her mouth yawn open and her shoulders shrink back in horror. Then she covered her mouth with the back of her hand. I could see her biting on her knuckles.

"She was murdered, strangled." I simplified the story for her. She didn't need all the details. I let her nurse her horror for another ten seconds and then told her, "These are ugly people you're involved with. I have to know everything you can tell me about them."

She didn't have anything extra to give me beyond what I already knew. She had come north to take Nancy Carmichael away from the beauty pageant. That was all she knew. She had met Nancy but did not know her whole name. Her group had been assured by Margaret, the same middle-aged Margaret my prisoner had met, that Nancy was sure to win. And then they would take her away and it would be a moral lesson to all the male chauvinist pigs who stood around and lusted for her beauty. And then Billie would strip and parade up and down to make the message even clearer. Billie had not wanted to do it. It had meant acknowledging to herself that she was as plain as a board fence, but she had overcome her reluctance and agreed, at Margaret's quiet insistence.

"Who was with you when they took your clothes?"

She wasn't sure. She had been driving the machine on which Nancy was a passenger. The other machines, one with two people on it, the other with one, had rendezvoused with them at the shelter. There had been no light except the headlights of the machines. She had only seen that the others were all wearing ski masks. She had simply fallen in behind them and followed obediently, through the woods and out over the ice. Then the lead machine had stopped and the driver had come back and asked her to strip. I didn't bother pressing for a description. It must have been the man Carl described. His assessment didn't fit either Nighswander or the two guys he'd had with him at the Lakeside. This was a fourth man. I wondered where the others were and if I should go back to the station and pick up a shotgun before I went after them. They were a murderous crew.

"You said they all undressed you. Did Nancy help?"

She thought about this for a moment. Probably her memory had slammed the door on the incident. She remembered it like a traffic accident, a sudden explosion of force and pain that had no edges to it beyond the dullness of the blows she had taken and the snatching of unknown hands.

"I don't think so. It was confusing, but I don't think she did. In fact, I'd say no." She rubbed her face with her left hand. "No, that's right. She stayed sitting on the machine where I'd left her, and then one of the other people got on in front of her and drove it away."

"Why did they do it? Were they punishing you for something? Had you done something to make them mad?"

She thought about it before answering. "I don't know," she said at last. "I just know I was certain I would die."

My own mind was bounding ahead. The only thing that fit my theory was that they had known I was following them and had wanted to slow me down. Any policeman would have done what I did, while they got away. I wondered only where they had been heading in such a hurry.

It was obvious that Nancy was to be hidden in a cabin or a cottage on the lake. My task was to find which one. The easiest way to do that was to try to round up help to assist in the search. I should call the OPP and have them seal the roads a few miles north and south of the Murphy's Harbour side road. Then I'd know I had the girl and the gang bottled up and I could look for fresh skidoo tracks at any cabin and go calling. I could find Nancy Carmichael by morning, with luck. But first I had to take care of this one. If the stove went out she would be dead in a couple of hours. She needed clothes and proper shelter. What I had done for her so far was first aid, nothing more. It didn't solve the major problems. She had to be dressed and locked in my nice warm slammer alongside my other prisoner before I could do any more hunting.

I explained it to her. "I want to take you to the mainland where you'll be warm. The first thing is to find you some clothes to travel in."

Her voice raced up into a near scream. "You're not going to leave me? Please? Please?"

"Just for ten minutes. There's a cottage on an island close to here. I'll break in and bring you back some clothes. Ten minutes is tops."

She was weeping again in panic. "What if they come back?"

That was when I made the decision to leave her my gun. As a professional, dealing with killers, I needed that gun, but this girl needed it more. "There's a gun in the right-hand pocket holster. Can you feel it?"

She dug her hand into the pocket and nodded.

"Good. All you have to do is point it and pull the trigger. If somebody comes back and tries any rough stuff, just do what I said and they'll go away."

If she was cool enough to point the gun properly they would go away for keeps, but most amateurs are too frightened of guns to use them for the money.

She shuddered, not a gesture but a deep-down tremble of dread. "I couldn't do that," she whispered.

"Remember what they've done to you, leaving you to die on the ice. If I hadn't come by, you'd be dead right now."

She lowered her face and I reached out and bumped her shoulder. "Don't worry. I'll be back before you can think."

She grabbed my arm. "Hurry," she said. "I'm frightened."

I left her squatting on the bench like a blue-coated monkey in some zoo. She thought she had problems. I knew I did. With no moon, nothing to steer by but the direction of the wind which had been steadily northeast the last time I'd had a chance to assess it against the shore line of the lake, I was gambling on finding a cottage soon. If I missed and began some crazy circling out of cold and desperation, I would be dead myself within an hour.

I stepped out, ballooned in warmth from the stove, but the cold knifed me within seconds. I had my gloves so my fingers were steady as I turned the key in the snow machine, but my teeth were clenched and about to chatter. Fortunately the machine started first click and I knelt in the saddle, pulling as low as I could behind the windshield, and headed slightly south of west toward the closest cottage on the lake, a big luxurious place built in the 1930s on an island about a quarter-mile from the ice huts.

I didn't force the speed. I was already getting rigid from cold and I didn't want to add a slip stream to the other problems. I kept the wind almost directly behind me, willing it to blow my machine down to the island, and I counted seconds. I figured I was doing fifteen miles an hour—that's four hundred yards a minute. I had counted to sixty-eight when the first rocks and trees flashed into the beam of my headlight.

I remembered that the cottage was on the southwest side of the island where it took the sun from morning on. I speeded up and zipped around, close to shore, thankful for the windbreak it made after I had rounded the southern tip.

The cabin was dark. I stopped at the foot of the wooden steps that led from the big stone dock to the verandah on the ground floor. By now I was so cold that my legs would hardly straighten. Like an old man I clambered slowly up, counting thirty agonizing steps.

The wind whistled across the verandah. I suppose I should have checked for footprints but my head was beginning to let me down. I was turning into a struggling survivor. Nothing mattered but warmth and shelter. I was ready to kill for it without thinking.

The door was covered by an old plywood screen door. I pulled it open and checked the door handle. It was secure, so I balled my fist inside my heavy glove and smashed the glass above the lock. I put my hand through and turned the handle from the inside. Something puzzled me as I did it, but I had no idea what it was and I pulled my arm back out and opened the door.

As I went through it I could feel a blast of warmth from the stove and I remembered a whiff of wood smoke on the wind outside. I should have worried, but I was too grateful for the heat until the languid voice said, "Well, aren't you a resourceful little nuisance."

56

7

A match popped. In the tiny wash of light it spread over the room I saw a man, his back turned negligently toward me, hands raised to the propane light on the wall. He lit the mantle and the room filled with light, soft and white and kind, seeming to help the warmth of the room soak into my face. The man lowered his hands and turned. It was Nighswander. He looked indolent, unafraid. I wondered if he was alone here or whether one of his friends was asleep in another room waiting to come to his assistance. Not that he would need much, not if he tackled me now. I was too stiff to react to an attack. He could break me like a china cup.

I decided to try a little bluff. It might buy me enough time to make my arms and legs supple again in the glorious warmth of the stove.

"Hey. Mr. Nighswander, right? Sorry about breaking in. I didn't know anybody was home." He looked about to speak but I pressed on, almost babbling. "You remember me from the Tavern, eh? I'm the p'lice chief. I don't generally go breaking windows but I gotta problem." I poured on all the northern Ontario roughness of accent. I wanted him to think I was a useless hayseed. Overconfidence on his part was the only break I could hope for if he swung at me. "Yeah, I gotta civilian out on the ice with a problem, came off his machine and broke his leg, it looks like."

He was still holding the match, letting it burn down almost to his fingers. Now he blew it out with a deliberate little puff. He turned and dropped the dead match on top of the stove, a square airtight Fisher. I edged closer, not into his striking circle but closer to the stove with its miraculous, softening heat.

"What happened to your parka?" He asked it in an amused tone, as if rehearsing the way he would tell the story to his friends later over white wine and squid and New Wave music.

"Shock. First aid, you know. I wrapped the guy up in it and came over to the nearest place to see if there's anything I can wrap him in, anything in the way of first aid stuff."

As I jabbered I was weighing up the room as a potential battleground. It gave me no advantages. There were couches along two of the walls and one armchair set close to the stove. Except for a bare coffee table and bookshelves, that was it. There was nothing to shove in his way, nothing heavy to throw, not even a rug under his feet that I could pull away. I looked him over, still grinning my big foolish grin. He was dressed as he had been in the Tavern, and I knew how he could move. His build was slim but square and hard. He worked out regularly, probably in a karate class. And besides, his muscles and joints were loose and limber. He would be hard to beat without the use of my gun, a quarter of a mile away in the ice hut.

I was about to go on but he held up his hand imperiously. "That's enough. I don't want to hear any more of this nonsense. I know why you're here. You're looking for the Carmichael woman."

"Howdya mean?" Being dumb was buying time and warmth. A high isolated corner of my mind considered his describing a seventeen-year-old as a woman and I decided I had been right. He had nothing to do with women.

"She's not here," he said. "But on the other hand, you are. You weren't supposed to get this far, Mr. Bennett. I'm going to have to stop you."

Slowly he took up his karate stance, moving as deliberately as if he were under water. I wondered if he was psyching himself to kill me.

I dropped the hayseed impression. "Stop me the way you stopped Katie?"

His pose slackened in surprise. "How did you find your way to her?"

"Easy. I just checked your room at the motel."

He sneered at me, as if I were slow. "I booked no room at the motel. I'm staying *here*."

"Well, somebody called Nighswander booked a room at the Muskellunge Motel, took a girl there, and killed her with a chop in the throat."

I was watching him but he gave no reaction. Instead he drew himself slowly up into the karate stance and nodded curtly to me.

"Don't try that judo crap," I warned him. "I'll shoot you."

He took a tiny step toward me. "Before you can draw your clumsy gun you will be unconscious." He said it through clenched teeth and I knew it was time to move.

I tried one last ploy, raising my left hand in a placating gesture while I sneaked my right to my back pocket and took hold of the knob at the top of my stick. "Hey, what's happening? I'm the police, you guys can't use that stuff to break the law."

It helped. He made his crouch a little more menacing, hissing between his teeth as he covered the next crucial yard between us. And in that first hiss I read the news that I could win. He was operating out of ego, not need. Break his ego and he would lie in a heap. I kept talking. I figured

59

I had a chance against a studio player. He had never done this for his life. Pain would throw him.

I made a show of backing off a foot, keeping him advancing as I drew my stick and flicked it underhanded in one movement. He threw up his hands instinctively, as I had known he would. A master would have ignored the stick and the pain unblinkingly, but this was an amateur. He was still good enough to kick automatically as he ducked. It almost connected, except that I had watched his weight shift and moved a half step to the left. As his foot flicked past my hip I followed through on my throw, forcing my arm forward and down into the center of his chest. He didn't even have time to groan. The dynamics of the action threw him away, twisting him back to his right from the doubled momentum of his kick and my counter. I knew the muscles in his groin and stomach would be torn. I had him beaten. But the fall took him into overkill, hammering his head onto the stove with a solid crunch that put him out cold.

I swore first but immediately thought better of it and allowed myself a grin. I was still stiff with cold. He should have minced me. But I had stopped him. I was proud of that much, at least.

I retrieved my stick and gave it a superstitious little pat with my left hand. I always respect things that help me. I wanted that stick to know I was in its debt again. Then I took out my handcuffs and cuffed Nighswander's right wrist to the wrought-iron log cradle. It was a solid piece of work, two four-foot circles of one-inch iron rod, one behind the other, welded together by a series of foot-long rods and loaded with heavy maple wood. He wouldn't get away from there until I came for him or his friends brought a hacksaw and took half an hour to saw him free.

Next I took my flashlight and searched the cottage. There was nobody there and no indication that anybody else had been there that evening. There was a snowmobile outside

60

the back door but it was snowed in, and I judged Nighswander must have ridden here immediately after leaving the Tavern, which complicated the question of who had killed the girl at the motel. I didn't stop to ponder. There was a good down parka, probably his, on a hook in the hall. I took it and a pair of snowmobile pants and a couple of blankets from the bedroom for the girl to wrap her feet in. Finally I brought water from the kitchen and bathed Nighswander's temples until he came around, groaning.

I knelt on his uncuffed hand while I questioned him, but he said nothing except to swear. After a few moments I gave up and went on with my biggest priority, rescuing the girl from the fishing hut. Afterward I would return here and find out more, but her life was in my hands, she had to be handled first.

I put on the parka, which was a little tight, rolled the blankets and pants together, and went back to the skidoo. I tucked my bundle under my right foot and knelt up to drive back along my tracks to the snow hut. It was easier to find than the cottage had been. The wind was as strong as ever and just as dense with snow, but as I headed into it I could smell wood smoke from the stove in the fishing hut. I followed it to its source in less than a minute and drove the machine up until its headlight was shining through the rear window. I came around to the door and crouched and called, "It's the police chief, open up." There was a long pause and I waited and did nothing. I didn't want to be shot with my own gun. At last the door eased open and the girl said, "Come in, Chief, I'm okay."

It was warm inside. She had been stoking the wood into the stove as fast as it could take it, acting out of fear and cold. I wondered how much longer her supplies would have held out. I pushed the bundle of clothes into her hands. "There's skidoo pants in there—put them on and give me my parka back." I turned away and wriggled out of the parka I'd brought from the cabin. I felt uneasy in the ice hut. It was too simple a spot for an ambush. If anyone wanted me stopped permanently, they could do it now from thirty yards away in this snow and I would never know they were out there until the bullets ripped through the walls. As an ex-Marine, I know you never occupy known positions, you move on before you consolidate. That way the mortar shells come pounding in behind you, not on top.

The girl changed smoothly and modestly, slipping into the ski pants first, then turning away to shuck my parka and put on the new one. She turned to me then, crouched on her bench, her head almost scraping the center of the roof. "How's that?" she asked perkily.

"Very fashionable. Now wrap up your head in the blanket, then your feet, and I'll bring the machine to the front door." I turned away, glad to be wearing my own parka with the familiar weight of the gun in the right-hand pocket. If I needed more help tonight, the Colt would be there.

I chugged the machine around to the door, turning it back to face the mainland. The girl came out, almost on hands and knees, shuffling like a Chinese bride in her constricting blanket. I sat her side-saddle on the machine in front of me, then wrapped the last folds of blanket around her feet. She nodded and slid one hand free of her parka sleeve to give me a little thumbs-up signal, and I knelt up and drove slowly back to the nearest point of the shore line, almost due west. Now that I was no longer pursuing other machines, I was more careful. Skidooing over ice can be dangerous, particularly on our lake, which is part of an ever-flowing chain connected by locks. The ice is weak in places where the current is fast. And even the flat areas can heave in pressure cracks that sometimes drift open a few feet, wide enough to swallow a snow machine whole.

As I drove I watched for ridging that would warn me of a weak spot. When I found one I stopped the machine, leaving the girl hunched behind the windshield. "Stay there, I have to test," I said. Then I slipped my stick out of my pocket, keeping the strap around my wrist, and lay flat out on the ice to check the gap at arm's length. I tapped until I was sure there was a gap of only about six inches between the two surfaces and that the slick of new ice, perhaps an inch thick, was continuous between them.

I got back on and told the girl "Hold tight!" then drove the machine around in a big circle, picking up speed and coming to the gap at full throttle. There was a jolt as we passed over and I slowed back to normal pace and went on watching. I was anxious to be back at the station, thinking about the case rather than my own survival.

Nobody had been to the station since I left and my skidoo tracks were well drifted in. I wondered how much more snow was going to fall. We already had ten new inches and more was layering down every second. It was a worry. If I went out again I might get the snow machine bogged. Those things aren't magic carpets. They need firm footing or they're liable to sink right into drifts and start cavitating. It was something else to worry about but first I wondered how Val Summers and my prisoner were.

They were fine. Val had taken the plastic seal off the thermostat and cranked up the heat a notch so the station was gloriously warm to come into. And there was fresh coffee. She hadn't slept but had been talking to the prisoner, woman to woman now the limelight was off and the prisoner was feeling a bit foolish.

I asked Val to stay out back with the first girl while I drank coffee with the second one. In the full light she turned out to be a dish. She was five-six, one-fifteen, blonde hair, even the makeshift outfit I'd scored for her didn't hide a real sexual confidence. I guessed she was the C.L.A.W. member who had worked as a model. I also guessed that it wouldn't take long to turn her off her man-hating, she seemed too warm a woman for lifelong separation from us all.

She had the same story as the first girl. This mysterious Margaret woman had contacted her after a hearing at the

Ontario Civil Rights Board. She had been protesting harassment by her employer, a fashion-house proprietor who reckoned his models should do their bit for corporate earnings by putting out for his out-of-town buyers. She had kneed him and taken her complaint to the government. He had turned up for the hearing in a wheelchair hired for the occasion, with his wife as character witness, and the case had been dismissed. Whispering through his pain, her employer had told her there and then to look for another job. She was in a boiling fury at him and all other men and had been inducted into C.L.A.W. It might not have stuck in her case except that the fashion industry is a small circle and she found herself unable to get more modeling anywhere. On top of that, her former boss was out of his wheelchair the next morning, taking off for Miami with, for once, his lawful wedded wife.

"So what was your job this evening? I already know the Carmichael girl was in on it and didn't need dragging away. What did you do?"

"I drove the getaway truck." She cocked her head to one side and her sweetly blonde hair fell sideways down to her shoulder. She beamed at me like a little girl who had remembered the right text in Sunday School.

"You understand the vehicle was stolen."

She pulled her head erect at once and tried to look less amused. "I was told we had the use of it for the evening."

"You did. But the owner never knew it. So when you reached the highway, what happened?"

She looked at me for a long moment. You could almost see the chess pieces moving behind her eyes. I had saved her pretty bacon out there on the ice, but I was still a Male Chauvinist and doubly a Pig, the enemy. She wondered what she owed me. I reminded her. "You could have been the second victim of the evening if I hadn't stopped. Somebody already strangled your buddy at the Muskellunge Motel."

64

Her eyes filled with tears. It was more impressive than screams or sobs. They were the honest tears of somebody for a friend you won't see again. "Poor Katie," she whispered. "Who would do that to her?"

"That's what I'm trying to find out. Who did she come up here with?"

"She said she was coming up with her boyfriend. She was driving, he wanted her to, but he was paying everything."

"That's no big deal—a few gallons of gas, a motel room."

"It was to her. Her husband never put out a nickel for her. She thought this guy was marvelous."

"Did you ever meet him?" I wanted facts, not True Romance. This was a murder.

She shook her head. "We were going to meet him tonight. He was going to be at the rendezvous with Nancy and Margaret."

"And where was that?"

She shook her head again, sadly. I think she would have told me had she known. Now she was warm and safe she realized how close she had been to death. "I'm sorry. I just don't know, we were never told."

"So all right, tell me where you went after the kidnapping." I already knew the first moves and it was a cold trail anyway, but I hoped it might have some kind of pattern to it, like a child's dot-to-dot puzzle. Maybe with some more information I could infer where the others fit in.

"Katie was waiting for us at the highway in the big wagon. Rachael and Nancy and I got in and went back to Katie's cabin."

"That was number six? And Katie was driving a big Ford wagon?"

She nodded impatiently. "Cabin six. But only Katie went inside. Rachael and I and Nancy went to another one that had been rented for us by Rachael's boyfriend."

"Was his name Nighswander?"

"I don't know." She almost shrieked it. Her eyes blazed. "Believe me, if I knew, I would say."

"Did you go into this other cabin?"

"Yes, we all did, and Nancy took off her silly swimsuit and put on some street clothes."

"What kind of clothes—a skirt, a suit, what?"

I might have guessed. Like all good man-haters, Nancy Carmichael had put on blue jeans. "With an Aran sweater, oyster-colored." On top of which she had put on her skidoo boots and her three-thousand-dollar designer coonskin coat.

"Then what happened?"

"That was our part of the exercise completed. Rachael and I left the cabin and walked out front. We were picked up there by another car. A man was driving."

"What did he look like?"

She shrugged. "It was hard to see, there was almost no light. I would have said he was under thirty and not very big or very heavy. But he had a wool hat on and I couldn't see much of his face or hair color or anything."

He might have been one of the three men at the Tavern. I stopped and counted bodies. If Nighswander was part of this, then I had three men against me—two now, with him handcuffed to the log box, as well as the two surviving C.L.A.W. people, Margaret and Rachael. That meant a minimum of four. Three of them had gone with Nancy Carmichael across the ice. That left one wild card somewhere. I wondered where. I needed help, that much was certain.

"Where did he drive you?"

She frowned. It was her first artificial gesture. It looked the kind of move she made when men asked her to do things she wasn't crazy about. "We went back down the highway, the way we'd been, and past Murphy's Harbour."

"You're sure of that?"

"Positive. Rachael pointed out the Toyota. It was where I'd left it, and we all laughed."

"And you stopped where?"

It was as I had begun to guess. There's a provincial campground just south of the turn-off. They had driven there and pulled into the parking lot.

"The car got stuck but the driver called it some bad names and managed to get through the snow and into the center."

"What happened then."

"There were two snowmobiles there. Somebody had taken them off a trailer."

"How do you know?" If she were right, the trailer might still be there, perhaps with a license plate on it that would lead me into the middle of this tangle instead of bouncing around the edges.

"Just observation. It had gone, but I could see where it had been driven away. Like, you know, there were two sets of tire tracks—the car, and then the trailer tracks smaller and over the top.

"You're very observant, noticing something like that." I kept my voice neutral. The comment could have been either a compliment or a sneer. She took it as a compliment. I was beginning to like her better than the other C.L.A.W. member.

"Wasn't I, though? The thing was, nobody was there for a couple of minutes. We wondered whether to stay in the car or look around. I was looking for footprints to see if anybody had been there recently."

"And had they?"

"Yes. Margaret was there. She was sheltering in the privy but she came out when she saw we'd come."

"You're sure it was Margaret?"

"Oh yes. She was all dressed up in a skidoo suit and red ski mask but I could tell it was her. There's a big street light in the middle of the lot. You know."

I plodded on through the story, taking her back over parts she didn't remember the first time. It took ten or fifteen minutes, and by the end I knew that the three women had been joined by Nancy and a man on another snow machine. The car took off then, back north toward the Murphy's Harbour cutoff. The man who had brought Nancy back took the driver aside first and talked to him and then came back to the women. My new prisoner, whose name was Freda, "Freddie" to the cell members of C.L.A.W., had taken one machine with Nancy on the back. They had followed the other two across country, over the frozen marsh and through the woods to the shelter I had found earlier. The other three people had left them there for half an hour and then returned and led them on across the lake to the ice huts. At that point they had stopped and undressed Freddie and left her. She did not know why, but I was becoming certain that it had been solely to prevent my catching up with them. They had seen my lights behind them. None of it was much help. I thanked her anyway and said, "I'm going to have to lock you up, along with your friend from the dance. It's no fun, but it's safer than that ice hut."

She was sitting across the desk from me and she stood up slowly. I thought she was going to protest but instead she stretched out her hand to me. I took it and she pressed it.

"If you weren't the heat, I'd kiss you," she said matter-of-factly. She was looking at me calmly and I realized that she meant every word.

"Save it. You'll hate my guts by the time you come to court on Monday," I told her. She laughed and shook her head.

"I don't think I will, but right now I'm saying thank you."

"Part of the service," I said. I had more on my mind than flirtation. I had seen Nighswander with two other men. Neither of them fit the description of the guy who had wrecked Carl's house and abandoned this girl on the ice. I was guessing he was also the man who had murdered the girl in the cabin. He was a killer, not a big-city limp-wrist, and I had to get back out into the snow and go look for him.

8

I locked her away and called Val out into the front of the station to bring her up to date on what had been happening. She was afraid. The situation was heating up. The tension had awakened the bad moments from the time her husband had been killed. Like most people she did not realize that evil is almost always selfish and casual. The people involved in giving pain don't consider their victims as people, they don't climb outside their own heads at all. They do whatever they want and are puzzled when the judge or some social worker asks them how they could have done it. Val had swallowed that fact along with the last of her tears for her husband, and now she was tasting its bitterness.

I promised to be back as soon as I could and I took down the station shotgun and checked the load. "You've got Sam. He can disarm anybody in a flash. And you've got the gun. If you want, I'll call the Legion and have some old soldier come down here and stick around," I offered.

"They're probably too drunk to know what's happening." She tried a tough little grin. "Don't worry. I'll be fine."

I kissed her on the nose and winked at her. "Right back. I'm going to follow up those tracks." I knew she was right about the men from the dance. If I asked for one I would get twelve, and they would be in no shape to do much more than blunder around roaring. I would move quietly and more efficiently on my own.

The wind was blowing just as hard and the snow was sifting down fine as flour. There's a local saying, "Little snow—big snow," and tonight was proving the point. We were going to end up with two feet before the night was over. I tramped back through the big drift to the garage behind the station. There was a five-gallon can of gasoline there, and something even more important—my snowshoes. I brought them out to the machine, topped up the gas tank, and clipped the snowshoes each side of the seat on the brackets I'd had installed. If the machine broke down, I would be able to tramp back over the snow without dying of exhaustion.

I cruised back into town, staying in the middle of the road. The force of the wind had drifted snow over much of the track I'd made a quarter-hour earlier, and I wondered how much I would find on the icy trail I'd been following when I encountered Freddie. But I had a hunch the others had been heading straight for shelter. And that meant I was looking for one of only a dozen or so cottages in a straight line from the last track I had been following.

I ran through town, past the Tavern, past the marina, past the line of ice sculptures that had been built during the week. The sculptures were obscured by snow, but I could pick out Carl Simmonds's effort, an eight-foot Mickey Mouse, and I grinned. Trust Carl to do something other than madonnas and snow queens and castles. He would win tomorrow. It might give him some consolation for the wrecking of his home.

I decided to follow my hunch. I would retrace my track out to the ice huts, then head north from there until I found a cottage with snowmobile activity around it. When I did, I would break in and check. It would mean I would lose the case in court. In a warm room, miles and months removed from the reality of tonight, some smooth lawyer would pillory me for violating somebody's rights. But I didn't care. I wasn't out to win cases or popularity contests. I wanted Nancy Carmichael safe. Let the lawyers scream. The people of Murphy's Harbour would back me up. They'd done it before.

I ran up the road around the lake, to the point where I had come up out of the bush and headed for town. I ducked back through the trees and out onto the ice. Going on instinct and my knowledge of the lake, I drove out to the ice huts where I had found the girl. By now the snow had been falling long enough to obliterate most of the skidoo tracks I had found earlier. Without them to follow I was more careful, remembering now what the locals had taught me about the ice in this area. Somewhere above the narrows, close to the place where the C.L.A.W. people had taken to the lake surface, there was a long open section. Some quirk of the current prevented it from freezing completely, although occasionally a treacherous inch or so of ice would cover the gap. Murphy's Harbour people referred to it as "The Cut" and could name the last dozen or so men to go through it. Most of them had been snowmobilers, but one Indian trapper had gone through and so had an exuberant drunk who had driven his pickup out to the ice huts and then had attempted to take a short cut back to Murphy's Harbour. He was still down there somewhere, in his steel coffin; the divers had never managed to locate him.

But I was confident now that I was heading north, away from the cut. I thought ahead as I drove, remembering which cottages lay on this course and what I knew about their owners. I drew the map of the lake in my mind, marking out any places that were winterized. I had checked them all a week ago, making sure none had been broken into. Some were still in use—a group of four or five on the east side of the

71

lake, just south of the narrows, and another one on Frog Island. And that was the recollection that made me reach forward and switch off the headlights.

There was one cottage on the island, a big rambling clapboard place like a beach house on Cape Cod. It stood on a rock at the southeast corner of the island. What made it important was the owner, someone I had met once last September on a morning I had paddled my canoe up there along the reed beds. The owner had been out in a solid flat-bottomed little boat with a Remington pump-action shotgun and a limit of mallards. Duck season was open, the sight was not surprising except for one detail. The owner was a woman and she fit the description both C.L.A.W. members had given me of their society's matriarch.

I swung my snowmobile half left on a course that would take me three hundred yards downwind of the island, far enough from it that they would never hear my motor above the roaring of the wind. I reached forward and switched off the headlight so nobody would see me coming and dropped my speed. Now that I no longer had to follow tracks it was easy to drive. I watched ahead for bumps or holes and steered by the pressure of the wind coming at me from my right. My eyes soon adjusted to the darkness. The dark was almost worth being free of the hypnotic corkscrewing of the snow coming into the headlight. And suddenly the black whale-bulk of trees loomed on my right front quarter.

I coasted to a stop, put the key to the engine in my pocket, and unclipped my snowshoes from their brackets. I didn't need them on the hard surface of the ice so I tucked them under my arm until I came to the first long drifts in the lee of the trees. The snow had gathered into tapered piles that would have been pretty in bright sunlight if I'd been carrying a camera instead of a Colt .38 in my gloved hand.

I went around the island into the teeth of the wind until I reached the edge of the marsh that gave the place its name. All the frogs were four feet under the ice right now, oblivious to the cold. I almost envied them as I pushed my gun back in my pocket and crouched to slip my boots into the snowshoe bindings. I use Indian-style attachments, loops cut from an old truck inner tube. They don't look as fancy as the leather buckles you get when you buy new snowshoes from Canadian Tire, but you can slip them over your boots without taking your gloves off, and that's worth any esthetics you have to sacrifice. Besides, you can slip them on or off in seconds.

The drifts were up to eight feet high behind the rocks on the edge of the marsh, but I stamped up over the top of them, sinking in less than knee deep. By the time I reached the old snow on top of the rocks I was sinking only a couple of inches. The snow was thinner there and my snowshoes snagged every few steps in the blueberry bushes underneath. I lifted my feet higher and placed them more carefully, but still stumbled. I swore as I fell, but in the same instant I saw the wicked orange eye of a muzzle flash wink at me from a window of the cottage.

I hit the snow rolling, all my soldier's instincts taking over automatically. It was harder in my parka than it had been in my combat fatigues in Nam and the snowshoes were almost impossible to turn, but I shucked them quickly and tossed them against a tree where I would be able to find them again if I had to.

All this took about ten seconds. I jumped up and ran four steps before pitching myself down and rolling again. A bullet sang off a rock behind me and scythed its way through the branches of the pine trees.

I was below the ridge of the rock now, too low for anyone at the window to aim at me. But whoever was there fired again. I listened to the sound and assessed the weapon. It

73

sounded like a heavy rifle, possibly a .308, big enough to kill a bear, plenty big enough to finish me. I crawled monkey fashion along to the left, toward the back of the cabin. The snow yielded under my hands and I was nose down in the coldness of it. I snorted quickly, blasting it away from my eyes and mouth. I was cold enough already, I didn't need any more problems.

The crawl brought me to a point in line with the corner of the cottage. It would have been impossible for anyone to hit me from the first position from which I'd been fired on. There was only a small window beside the back door and it looked as if there was not much room inside to maneuver a long gun.

I crouched there for a moment, running over my alternatives. I tried the first one and it failed. "Police. Chief Bennett. Stop firing!" I shouted. In return I got a high angry shout that I couldn't understand and two more shots, which I could. I stayed low and thought some more.

It seemed to me that the person inside was alone. Otherwise someone else would have moved to the back window and taken a shot at me from there. Of course, there was a chance that the second person was there but didn't have a gun. Then I remembered the Remington pump the woman had used. I wasn't anxious to take any chances against a cloud of shot, even bird shot.

I checked my surroundings as my night vision improved, the way it does under stress. There was a stack of firewood under a tarpaulin against the back door. I thought for a moment about tossing a log through a window, then racing to a different one while the rifleman followed his reflexes. It didn't make sense. I couldn't just dive through the window. I might go headlong into the stove or down the cellar steps or break my head against a table. I had to bring the people inside the cottage out. And I had to do it now. I couldn't run for help. That would take hours. The gunman would be gone, possibly forever. And another thing. Ever since Nam I have had a hatred of being shot at without returning fire. In combat, it would have been simpler. I would have rolled up alongside the window and tossed in a couple of grenades. After the explosion I would step in and hose down anything that still moved. Then consolidate, a few meters beyond the house.

I lay and pondered what I could use instead of grenades and the M16s of the other guys in the team. And as I lifted my head for a cautious glance, a sudden downshift in the wind filled my nostrils with the smell of burning hardwood. Of course! The place was heated by a stove.

Keeping low, I ducked behind the woodpile. Like most cottage woodpiles up here it was made up of neat birch logs cut from trees thin enough that the logs did not even need splitting. Each was about eighteen inches long. I eased three of them out of the back of the pile and stuffed them into the front of my parka, flinching as the wind struck through the open front. Then I ducked past the pile to take a look alongside the west side of the cottage. I was in luck. There was a maple, rare this far north, against the house. No doubt it had been left there because it added to the charm of the place. There was even a bird feeder hanging close to the house.

I thought for a moment. The feeder meant there was a window there, which could mean another gun. I knelt and drew out one of my birch logs. I threw it with all my force against the back door. It clattered there like a clumsy attempt to break in. Without waiting, I stumbled through the snow to the maple and swarmed up the trunk on the side opposite the cottage. The thickness of the tree might just save me from a first shot. I clenched my stomach muscles instinctively against the possible deadly crash of a bullet from the hunting rifle. None came. Within seconds I was above eye level from the window and swarming out on a branch that overhung the roof. Snow flopped off the branch onto the roof and I kept going, hoping nobody inside would hear it above the wind and guess what it meant.

The branch bent under my weight, bowing down within three feet of the roof, about ten feet below the crest. I let myself down gently onto the roof, praying that my weight would not start an avalanche and warn those inside that an ex-Marine was trying to take the high ground. As I touched the roof I began to slide but kept hold of the branch and used it as a lever to inch my way up to the peak. The chimney came out through the center and I made for it. The round, insulated metal pipe warmed my face with glorious heat as I sat there straddling the peak.

The chimney was covered with coarse chicken wire to discourage birds or raccoons from exploring while the owner was away. It was a problem for me but I pulled out my clasp knife, holding my right glove in my teeth as I sawed through a few strands until I could fold the wire back out of the way. The heat was intense but I managed the job without dropping knife or glove. I snapped my knife shut and slipped it into my tunic breast pocket and pulled the gloves on quickly. My hand was blistered but I didn't care. I knew now that I could win.

The birch logs in my parka were not quite big enough for my purpose. I thought for a few seconds, debating what to do, then tugged off my fur hat and held it in my teeth while I flapped up the hood of my parka and snapped it as tightly as it would go around my face. This was no time for frostbite. I slipped my log into the hat and quietly forced it into the chimney. The heat and smoke stopped at once and I eased myself backward until I was straddling the roof at the back of the house. So far I was lucky. Nobody had heard me. But when they realized what was happening they might try to loosen things up by blazing a few rounds through the roof, hoping to pierce the chimney and put themselves out of the misery I was causing. I didn't want to be in the way. I wanted to be Br'er Rabbit, sitting in the clear, waiting for things to develop my way.

It took almost ten minutes. I sat patiently, my head bowed so the wind struck the top of my hood and was deflected from the bare skin of my face, my hands tucked under my armpits for warmth. I was cold in the legs and feet, but it was bearable.

The break came as I had expected, with two quick shots up through the roof. One of them caught the edge of the chimney and weannggggged away harmlessly. And then I heard a commotion at the front door. I pulled out my last piece of birch and threw it just past the edge of the roof so it fell on the verandah in front of the door. It clattered down on some bare spot where the snow had not settled. The commotion stopped. Then came the sound I had been waiting for, glass breaking at the side of the house next to the maple I had climbed. I strained my ears in the wind and heard the gasping and coughing of a person starved for air. I guessed that he thought he would try to fool me by staying away from the doors, but when the window hadn't opened, he had panicked and smashed it.

I cocked my leg over the roof and made myself into a toboggan, sliding down the roof to the edge where I caught my heel in the eaves trough, stopped, turned over onto my stomach, and dropped the rest of the way to the ground. I saw the head sticking out of the window and grabbed it, pulling the person out until he was rocking over the sill on his stomach.

"Try anything and you're dead," I said in a low voice. He squirmed helplessly and I hoisted him the rest of the way over the sill, out of the thick smoke that poured out around him, choking me even outside in the air. It was not until I had finished blinking away the tears that I realized who I was holding.

9

It was Irv Whiteside, his face blackened with smoke, the lapels torn away from his natty suit where I had hauled him out over the glass shards in the bottom of the window frame. I gave him thirty seconds to grab some air, then asked him, "What the hell gives?"

He held up both hands, still coughing as the words glugged out of him. "I didn't know, Reid. I didn't know it was you, honestagod. I thought it was them bastards back to get me."

I wanted more but he was shuddering with cold. I had to get him inside. "Is there anybody else in there?"

"No. Just me."

"Good. Stay here." I shinned back up the tree and out over the roof, leaving him collapsed against the wall, spitting soot and smoke. It was easier on the roof now I did not have to worry about making a noise, and within thirty seconds I had my plug out of the chimney. The hat was scorched and the burnt fur lining smelled like hell, but I kept it in my hands as I slid back down the roof and dropped beside Whiteside. I wasn't thinking of him as Irv right then. This was no friend. Not after shooting at me.

He was twitching uncontrollably with cold and I had to lead him to the back door. It was locked, but I booted it once at lock level and we were inside. Irv stayed by the door as I crouched low to the floor and followed the dull beam of my flashlight through the brown cloud to the stove, holding my breath all the way. I opened the stove door wide and I could see the smoke pulling in and up the chimney, like bath water going down a drain. There was a pile of pine kindling wood next to the stove and I threw a handful in. It burst into a bright cleansing flame that pulled more and more smoky air away. Within a minute or so the air was breathable again and I was able to shut the back door and move Whiteside in where it was properly warm. There was an oil lamp on the table and I lit it. In the dull light with its smoke haze Whiteside looked like some character from an old Dutch painting. But he was able to breathe again and I started asking my questions.

"Why are you here?"

"I was hired as a bodyguard for the kid."

"Which kid?"

"Nancy Carmichael."

"Who hired you and what did she need a bodyguard for, anyway?"

It came out slowly, the way most stories do under interrogation. He forgot, and backtracked, but finally I got the facts. I was sure they were the facts.

It all boiled down to Nancy Carmichael's sense of the dramatic. She knew the C.L.A.W. people were going to bring her to this cottage. She was certain she would get away with the gag and planned to stay here until Monday while I searched the motels on the highway and put the OPP and the rest of the outside world on the lookout for her.

That still left two questions unanswered. "If she was among friends, why did she need a bodyguard, and why the hell were you shooting at me?"

It seemed that Nancy was not just a pretty face. She had brains enough to realize that as a rich man's daughter she might be a valuable commodity once she stepped outside the law and disappeared. She knew Irv from years of coming up to Murphy's Harbour, mostly without her father, who was too busy to spend more than occasional weekends at the family place on the lake. She had heard the local rumors about Irv Whiteside's past and had bought the glamor of it.

"Hell, you know, Chief," he apologized, "folks think it was like *The Godfather*, fer crissakes. I didn't tell her no different. She's a nice kid."

"You still didn't tell me why you were trying to kill me."

"Well, it's like this. I told the help I'd be upstairs, to close up and go home without disturbing me. They figured I had a broad up there. So I went down the firesteps and out to the marina. Like, I keep a skidoo there. That was it. I was out here by eleven, poured myself a snort, and waited. Around eleven-thirty they turn up. I can see right away they're excited. There's five o' them, not six, like I expected. So I open the door and they come stormin' in outa the cold but they're not laughing, like I figured. Nancy's cryin'. So I ask her what's up and she points to the big one who's wearing the ski mask and she says, 'He stripped one of the girls and left her on the ice to die.' So I say to him, because this is a him, this is no broad. I say, 'What's going on?' and he says, 'Keep outa this.' And I say I'm goin' to keep the kid with me and the rest of them can go. But he just sighs, real weary. He says, 'I thought some dumb bastard would try that,' and he pulls a gun on me. He says to me, he says, 'One move outa you and you're through worryin' about anythin'.' Then he grabs Nancy and they all go back out to their machines and away. I go through this place and find the rifle but when I go down to the dock they've screwed up my skidoo. So I lie low to wait for morning, but I'm scared and I'm goddamn mad. So I keep the lights off and my eyes open. And when I see somebody coming over the rocks, sneaking up, instead of up from the dock like a normal person would've, I figure it's the guy with the gun back again and I let fly."

I thought about what he'd told me. On the face of it they had been dumb, leaving Irv here with a rifle, but as I thought it through I could see sense in their plan. For one thing they weren't sure how many more people Nancy had told, including possibly me. Leaving him here, angry and armed, had given him a chance to shoot me if I turned up and left them with the choice of taking Nancy to some place nobody knew about. It seemed to me they were adjusting their plan as they went along, and that made it harder to second-guess them.

My face was burning. I realized it had been frostbitten when I was up on the roof. Tomorrow it would be swollen and blotchy. Tonight it was pins and needles but I didn't care. It was the only thing about me that was really alert. I felt dull and outwitted, trying to keep up with the chain of events Whiteside had described. I rubbed my face with two fingers until I got used to the pain, then I asked him,

"Did Nancy give you any idea where they were going, except for here?"

"No. Honest, Chief. This place belongs to the woman who set up the kidnapping. Calls herself Margaret Sumner."

The name meant nothing to me. I pushed him. "What do you know about her? Is she a dumpy broad, in her fifties?"

He nodded, eager as a puppy to please. "That's her. There's no Sumner on the Reserve, that's for sure, but she's an Indian, around fifty-five."

I remembered the September morning. Three bangs of the pump gun, three ducks. Maybe she was Indian, but if so she had made money along the way. Her clothes were expensive.

"Anything else? Is she married, widowed, what?"

He held up his hands. "That's all I know. She bought this place last summer. I've seen her come into the marina a time or two, keeps an old plywood runabout there, got a Mercury motor."

I sensed a pattern to this. She had bought the cottage here

and then set about building her little organization. Had it been because she wanted to get her hands on the Carmichael kid for something? Or had the Carmichael kid seemed like a usable totem for her cause? Whichever it was, Irv Whiteside wouldn't be able to help me. I tackled his knowledge from the other end.

"How come you and Nancy Carmichael are so close? Are you getting next to her?"

He folded at the shoulders and crossed his legs guiltily. "Hey, come on, Chief, get real. Me an' a kid like that?"

"Well, how much was she going to pay you for looking after her?"

"Nothing." He muttered it, not looking at me.

"Nothing? You don't work for nothing, Irv. I've seen your sheet, don't try to snow me."

"This was a favor." The rawness of his longing for the girl was painful to watch. "I mean, she's a pretty kid. I'm a man of the world. You know. I'd be shut up here with her a coupla days. You never know what'll happen."

I slumped down in an armchair, weary beyond belief. "You mentioned pouring a snort. Is there any more around?"

"Yeah! Sure. You want some?" He was on his feet at once, desperate to please. He found the bottle. It was J & B.

"Sorry it's not Black Velvet, Chief. I'm a scotch man."

"Sounds good," I said. He found a couple of coffee mugs and poured a solid belt into both.

He gave me mine, then raised his and said, "Chimo!"

"Chimo yourself." I toasted him and sipped. It went down smooth and spread out into my tired body like fresh blood.

Now he was setting his drink down and feeling in his pocket for cigarettes. He found them in his side pocket, crushed flat from his exit through the window. He extracted one, rolled it gently, and lit it with a stick of kindling he then threw into the stove.

"Now." I sipped again and set down my drink. "You prob-

82

ably don't need me to say it, but I have to. You're in trouble up to your ass. For openers, you're a part of a conspiracy to commit a felony." I looked at him to see how he was taking it. The kidnapping was nothing more than a case of public mischief and that's just a misdemeanor, but I wanted him scared. And besides, the caper involved a murder now.

"What's more, you attempted to murder a peace officer." He put his drink down on the floor and spread his hands like a crucifixion victim. "Come on, Chief. I told you what was goin' down."

"You know as well as me that story wouldn't last a minute in court."

He said nothing, just sat staring at the floor. Slowly he lowered his hands and brought the right to his mouth for a drag on his smoke. He cupped the cigarette in his hand. He had never been in the pen but he had worked for men who had. He knew the drill. No J & B, no Friday night women, just noise and fear and the chance of ending up as somebody's punk if you didn't hit any guy who looked at you sideways.

I took pity and got to the point. "So we'll scratch the shooting. I've been shot at before, by experts."

He looked up now, his eyes narrow as he considered the thin slice of hope I'd handed him. "And you're no part of the conspiracy, so we can scratch that as well . . . for a price."

"You mean you'd forget about everything." His voice was quiet. He spoke almost without moving his lips, a criminal again.

"I'm ready to."

"I'll pay whatever wants payin'." He made a half swoop toward his wallet but backed off when I looked at him.

"You know me better than that. What I need is some help. Hang in with me until this is over and I'll forget the rest of this nonsense."

He reached out his hand automatically, forgetting the

cigarette butt. As his fingers extended, the butt fell to the floor and he stepped on it firmly. I shook his hand. "This is going to be hard," I promised him. "These are tough bastards. They've already killed one woman and tried to kill another."

"Killed a woman?" His horror was genuine.

I filled him in briefly, including the bit about the girl on the ice, then asked, "Waddya say?"

"Let's get 'em," he said.

"Okay. First thing, I want to know all you can tell me about the plan. Start talking, give all the names and facts you've heard, all the details. So far, none of it is making much sense. Maybe you can put the pieces together."

There wasn't much. He had known about the plot for three weeks. Nancy had come up alone and stayed over at the Tavern, ostensibly to go cross-country skiing. She had confided in Irv. She thought the thing was a big joke and hoped there would be plenty of headlines because it might help her when she reached the Miss Toronto contest. She would go into that contest, as she had ours, because her father owned houses in both places.

I stopped him here. "She has to be nuts. Doesn't she know the Miss Toronto is always chosen at the Police Games? No copper would vote for a dingbat like her."

"She's no dingbat." Irv was just the safe side of angry. "She's real smart. She's already in college, at seventeen. She speaks French better'n Jean Arcand at the bait store."

"She's got a thirty-eight bust, Irv, and you never looked any further. She's also got a big mouth. If she was letting you in on this dumb plan of theirs, she must have told half the world. She's likely got a whole lot of other people involved, people with no connection with this C.L.A.W. outfit."

He said nothing. I guess he knew I was right, that he wasn't the only one with the kid's secret. But that's not what he wanted to hear. I believe he was in love with her. I softened my approach. I wanted him to help me from choice, not anger.

"Did she tell you anything about this group of hers?"

"She said they were a great group of women."

I set down my empty coffee mug and sighed. "That shows it's wide open. There's at least one guy with the group, maybe more. And the one you saw is a tough, mean sonofabitch."

Irv stood up, convulsively clenching his fists. They were big, a fighter's fists. I was glad he was on my side. "I'd like a couple o' rounds with that bastard."

"You'll get them," I promised. "And we've got to find him. Unless I'm badly off base, he's the guy who murdered the girl at the motel and left the other one to die on the ice. He pulled a gun on you. We've got to stop him."

Irv was pacing, making small chopping punches with both hands, working out his anger as if this were a gym and he were honing himself for a bout.

"Did Nancy say anything about her group, what it was for?"

"Not much." He was still chopping punches that could have cracked ribs. "Only thing she said was, it was a feminist outfit."

"Feminist, not just a women's group. You're sure?"

He frowned. Subtleties of politics weren't his line. "Sure I'm sure. Feminist is what she said."

That made a difference. Feminist groups drew support from left, right, and center, all the shades of political color there are to the left of the Ku Klux Klan. The thought made me angry. I'm supposed to keep the peace here. It's not in my charter to hammer people into the ground or shoot them or open their mail or any of the other things that activists worry about. But on the other hand, I am a one-man band, and if she was calling on some heavy-duty troublemakers I would have to break some more rules and earn some more bad black ink. It would be the only way I could prevent somebody from doing worse to some helpless member of the public. They would justify their actions in the name of "The People," whoever the hell *they* were, but mine would be the actions of a dyed-in-the-wool reactionary.

I stood up and pulled on my scorched and smoky-smelling hat. It didn't improve my mood. "All right, so security is shot full of holes. She's been talking and there's a good chance she's got some wild-eyed radicals on her side. We've got to get hold of her before they do anything crazy."

"Tonight?" Irv was startled. His plans had been for a couple more scotches and a few hours sleep, helping me with the rough stuff by daylight if he had to.

"Tonight." I confirmed his fears for him. "The weather's too bad for them to make a run for it down the highway. She will still be here in some cottage until the snow stops. After that, they could take her cross country on a skidoo and meet the road someplace."

Irv reached for his outdoor clothes, a one-piece skidoo suit, extra large, to cover his out-of-place gray suit. I waited while he dressed and pulled on big rubber boots over his shoes. "Have you got any more shells for that rifle?"

He patted the pocket of his skidoo suit. "I already put them in here."

"Load up. You may need that thing."

I left him doing that while I went out back to the tree where I had dumped my showshoes and slipped them on. Irv came out of the back door as I finished. "Wait here," I told him, and stumped out to my snow machine. It was standing in the center of its very own snowdrift, but it started first try. I brushed the snow off the seat and drove up to the front of the cottage. Irv came down the steps to meet me, plunging waist deep in one drift. He climbed on behind me and I asked him, "Which way did they take off?"

He pointed vaguely west and I started off that way, making a big loop first to my left, then right again until I picked up the trail. They had done their best to run Indian file so the track would be less obvious, but it was the only track on the lake not yet covered with new snow. I followed it toward the far shore through the hypnotic dazzle of the snow that was still falling as fast as ever.

The track led straight to the shore line, then turned north until it reached a big older place, one of the summer houses that had once belonged to some lumber baron or other. Right now I wasn't interested in history. I just knew it would be a pig to search, especially if the guy with the gun was alive and well and hiding somewhere inside. I would have given anything to have had Sam with me instead of Irv Whiteside.

I drove right past the place without stopping. Irv was bumping me on the back trying to get my attention, but I just held up my free hand to let him know I'd heard. This was no time for a frontal attack.

We stopped a hundred yards past the place and I switched off the lights and the motor and strapped on my snowshoes. It was hard to talk over the rushing of the wind, but when I was set to go I beckoned to Irv and he leaned close.

"I want to go round the back of that place with the tracks. How good are you with that rifle?"

"Not bad," he said automatically, then remembered I could prove different and added an apologetic, "Not usually, anyhow."

"Good. I want you out in front of the place, where you can see the top windows. Give me five minutes. Then loose off a round that hits the roof line. Don't shoot the window out, there may be some poor innocent bastard inside and you'll kill him. I just want you to get everybody diverted. Can you do that?"

He by God could. I patted him on the shoulder and said, "Count to five hundred." Then I jogged clumsily on my snowshoes over the lake snow and up the slope, about a hundred yards north of the cabin. I was lucky. The original rich owner had owned enough of the shore line that there was no other building around to confuse the issue. I cut through the wood, ducking under the snow-laden branches of the second-growth spruce near the shore. Then I was up on smooth rock at the level of the cottage. After my experience with Irv, I was careful to keep my silhouette always against the trees, even though the snow was so thick I could hardly have been seen anyway. The flakes stung my face, biting at me endlessly as if I were under a carefully directed dry shower.

It took me four minutes to get close to the cottage. The first thing I saw was a light in the window. I inched forward, checking for some sentry posted outside. That's where a soldier would have waited. But these people weren't soldiers. There was nobody there, no track in the snow. What was more, I couldn't see any snowmobiles on the back or north sides of the house. I would have checked all around but it was getting close to Irv's time and I wanted to be in position.

I waited the remaining forty-five seconds, hunched against the wind, blinking away the gritty snow. Then I heard the smash of Irv's rifle and the angry buzz of a ricochet off the high front of the house. There was a thirty-second silence, then a second shot, closer this time. Irv was creeping up on his target, letting off some of his anger by blasting the house.

I crept closer to the window and peeked in from a yard away. It would have been a dumb thing to do normally, but I could see no disturbance in the snow outside. Nobody had booby-trapped the window to snare eavesdroppers. The room was like the interior of a thousand other cottages. Heavy wooden furniture, propane lamps, two of them lit. A bookcase filled with the kind of soft-backed junk people read on holiday, a pretty good rack from a white-tailed deer. No people. I wondered if our birds had already been and flown. And if so, why were the lights burning? I kicked off my snowshoes, took out my flashlight, and went to the back door.

There was a heavy old screen door on the outside and I could tell from the pie-slice depression in the snow that someone had opened it that evening. It must have been an hour or so earlier, the depression was drifting in. And there were no footprints away from the door.

I stood and thought about that for a moment, wondering what had happened. Had someone inside made a run to escape, then been caught at the doorway and dragged back inside? It was not logical that anybody had come to the back door, there were no tracks there except my own. I flashed my light around in the snow as Irv loosed off his third round in front. I was looking for stains in the snow, a sign that some-one had emptied a coffee pot or a man had relieved himself here. But there was nothing. I straightened up and gave three long whistles through my teeth. After a couple of repeats, Irv responded and then came out of the snow, rifle at the ready.

"It looks like they've gone," I told him. "But they've been here, or somebody has, inside the last couple of hours. I'm going in."

"Good idea." He held the rifle in his left hand and swung his numbed arm against his side a couple of times. "I'm god-damn freezing."

He reached out for the storm door but I stopped him. "Don't touch it yet, I'm not sure what's going on here."

He shrugged, a vague, disinterested move in the dark. "You worry too much, y'ask me."

"It's kept me alive so far." I went around the corner of the cottage. There were no lights on this side, no disturb-ances in the snow, either. I crept up to the closest window, ducked under and past it, then reached up to the corner closest to the back of the house and shone my light in. Nothing happened. Nobody shot at my light. I relaxed a touch and straightened up to peer in and check the inside catches. I was lucky. It was a single-glazed casement made up of six panes of glass. I pulled my glove tightly on my right hand and punched out the pane closest to the handle. Then I reached in sideways to the window as I unfastened the catch. It was that turn that saved me. I was a narrow target, hunched into my fur hat, my collar raised right to the edge of the hat covering my entire bare skin from harm when the blast hit, showering me with broken glass from the remaining window panes. I fell to the ground, rolling instinctively close to the wall for shelter while my head unscrambled. My eardrums were saved by my leather hat but both ears were deaf.

I pulled off my right glove and drew my gun. Then I stood up and hoisted myself over the window sill into the room. In the flashlight beam I could see it was a bedroom and the door was blown in toward me, broken off its hinges. I guessed what had happened but ran forward anyway, through the familiar smell of explosive smoke into the kitchen. The back door of the cottage was flung in shreds around the room. Outside in the snow I could see the ruin of the storm door and the bloodstains that told their own story.

Irv Whiteside was dead. The blast had taken him waist high. One leg was severed, the other hanging by a clotted strand of flesh. His entrails were spread around him. I stood for a minute, playing my flashlight over him as if the beam were a magic wand that would put him back together again. Shocked as I was, I knew what had caused those wounds. He had walked into a booby trap, something triggered by opening the storm door. And by the mess he was in, I knew what had been the device at the heart of it. Those wounds came from a fragmentation grenade.

10

I've seen a lot of men killed. Some of them the same way as Irv Whiteside, literally blown away. But they were all guys who knew the odds. They didn't like them but accepted the thought that a mortar shell could land close enough to leave nothing behind but their boots. It didn't make things easier, they lived with fear the way civilians might live with toothache, but they weren't innocent the way Irv had been, the way a two-year-old is when it totters out onto a highway. It made his death more sad, made me more angry.

I brought him inside where the foxes and raccoons wouldn't insult his broken body any further. There was a plastic snow shovel leaning against the woodpile and I used it to pick up everything I could find. It took longer than I wanted. So did the task of slipping the hinge pins off an inside door and wedging it into place in the damaged door frame of the back door.

I began to concentrate on the people who had booby-trapped the cabin. If they had access to grenades they were part of something far better organized than C.L.A.W. It was impossible to know what their mission was, but it had nothing to do with winning free ink for Nancy Carmichael. And then I remembered, some of her father's money came from a company in Toronto. The company made missile systems, including one for the American missile that had brought out the peace-lovers on the city streets. Maybe the kidnapping was all a scam. Carmichael was the target.

I put the spread from the bedroom over the mess that had been Irv Whiteside and then stood for a while, looking down at the body and wondering what to do next. A million thoughts needled me, distracted me. I realized that the murderer must have fastened the grenade to the door frame with a line from the pull pin to the outside door. He had opened the outside door once to check how much line he needed so that a man would open the door without thinking, without enough time or light to recognize the clack when the lever flew away and the last four seconds of his life started. The murderer had planned it so the pin would be out and the fuse working while the person was still opening the door, his body fully exposed to the blast without even the inadequate pine boards of the outer door to shield him. The cloud of steel fragments would hit him from two feet away at waist height. A one-hundred-percent kill.

Slowly I moved Irv out of my mind and started assessing priorities. These people were professional haters. They had killed twice, almost three times. They would not hesitate to use Nancy Carmichael as a bargaining tool. They would not hesitate to kill her if they decided there was a need to do so. I had to find her right away. Nothing else mattered. Not revenge for Irv's death, not rest or sleep or extra armament. Nancy Carmichael was in real trouble and I was the only one who could save her.

I debated with myself before I reached that conclusion. I recognized that nobody would have blamed me for giving up, going to the phone and calling for help which would not reach me before noon at least, for going back to the Legion and bringing up a dozen volunteers, old men who weren't as able to handle the cold and exposure as I was. Doing that would have been logical and safe, and totally useless. No, I was on my own, without even Sam to help me. If the girl was in danger, and I thought she was, the danger was immediate. A delay would bring me to her after she was dead. I had to find her. But how? Were she and the others all somewhere along this row of cottages? Or had they gone out to the highway and the car the man had used to drive the two C.L.A.W. women to the park? Whichever it was, they were somewhere else while I stood in a rising smell of broken guts, handling the guilt for responsibility for Irv's death.

I checked the door one last time. It would not hold against a bear, but if I could get back within a day or so it would stay in place against the shoving of foxes or other vermin. I went out, opening the front door carefully in case it too was booby-trapped, and put on my snowshoes, which were lying in the snow.

Irv's footprints led me back to my machine and I started it, hunching down against the everlasting snow, still wondering what to do next. I had one real murderer against me and a couple of very tough women.

I started back, staying on the lake ice, the details chasing one another through my mind as endlessly as the beads on my mother's rosary. I needed someone to talk to. I have an assistant, a young Indian kid called George Horn. He's tireless and intelligent and eager, but this month he was tending his family's trap line. If he were here instead of curled into a shelter somewhere, it would be good to sit and thrash out possible scenarios, to try and make some sense of the night. I was too close to everything, the lead hound of the pack, so close to the fox's brush I couldn't see where I was heading. I needed perspective and I needed time, but there wasn't any time to spare.

I drove carefully, keeping to the east shore of the lake, far enough out to be clear of the weak patches of ice where springs bubbled out of the shallows, warming the water and thinning the ice above treacherously. The trees of the shore line broke the wind for me and I began to feel almost warm, drowsy. My chin was pulled down into the collar of my parka and the scorched leather hat was tight over my ears. I was tired and shaken, and the numbness that follows the death of a comrade, even a cherry guy you never got a chance to know, was pulling me into myself. I was traveling fast but time seemed extended, as if I were on some kind of high. Every thought seemed to take minutes to pass through my head and the machine seemed almost stationary, although I was clipping along at close to thirty, watching the ice surface ahead.

And then I realized what I had to do. It was my only chance and I would have done it earlier if I hadn't been so hell-bent to chase down the kidnappers along their own skidoo tracks. I turned the machine half right and pushed out over the center of the lake toward the cottage where I had left Nighswander. He would be conscious by now—sore, but able to talk. Maybe he wouldn't want to, but I was in no mood for playing games. If necessary, I would convince him.

I was running by guesswork, concentrating on my thoughts, and might have missed the whole island if I had not suddenly found myself staring at a crack in the ice dead ahead, a black break in the play-back of light from my machine as it bored through the corkscrewing snowflakes. I'd found the cut. I swung further right, and I must have run half a mile when I saw the trees loom in front of me. I had reached my island after all. As I approached it, still thirty yards clear of the crack in the ice, I recognized the configuration of the rocks at the south end, to my left.

I pulled in beside them, tucking the machine up close to the vertical surface where nobody could come at me as I put my snowshoes on. It's only in Roy Rogers movies that guys leap on other guys from fifteen-foot heights. It doesn't happen in the snow, in the dark. I was safe against my rock.

I took off my right glove and put my hand deep in my

pocket, cradling the .38 Colt. It would have been foolish to draw it, numbing my hand with cold. A quick draw isn't important. A clean, accurate shot is, and that would have been impossible with my fingers frozen. I did not use my flashlight. It seemed to me that the snow in front of the cottage was more broken than I had left it. It was not smoothed over the way it should have been after an hour or two of steady snow. That made me hesitate. Had they come here, too? Had they set up another frag trap for me? And if they had, would they have used the same mechanism? I kept low and made a complete circuit of the cottage. The light was still burning in the room where I had fought Nighswander and left him cuffed to the log box. No other lights were lit. I crouched by the back door for a few moments, wondering how best to go in.

At last I made my decision. I had an advantage that Irv Whiteside had never earned. I know grenades. I have thrown my share of them. I know you've got a count of four to get out of the way when the pin is pulled and the lever flies away. In four seconds I could be around the corner of the cottage and flat on the ground where splinters wouldn't hit me. I decided to try it.

There was a jumble of prints against the back door. I stood there a moment, weighing alternatives. Then I pulled off my snowshoes, laying them flat, out of harm's way, and grasped the handle of the door. With my guts clenched into a tight ball I slammed the door open and threw myself for the corner of the cottage, rolling as I fell, curling my body around the corner out of the way.

I had a whole second left. I waited, pulling tight into the snow, aware of the nonstop hissing of the new snow drifting down on me. Nothing happened. I waited thirty seconds, then stood up. This time I opened the door calmly. Then I pulled my flashlight and checked the crack in the door for any sign of a trip wire connected inside. I couldn't see one. It seemed to me that was the way they would have set the trap, using a string which would be tightened as the door opened. There are other ways, better ways, but trip wires are the closest thing to foolproof.

When I was sure there was no trip, I lifted the flap on the right side of my hat, leaving the ear exposed, drew my gun, and pushed the door open another foot with my knee. Nothing happened. No metallic click alerted me to dive for safety. Moving quickly, I slid in around the door and dropped into a low crouch.

I was in the kitchen of the cottage, in darkness except for the beam of my light. There was nobody here. Under the door I could see the faint orange wedge of lamplight from the room where I had left my prisoner. I pushed the flashlight back into my pocket and opened the door slowly and carefully, checking for devices. There was nothing to see and I slammed the door wide open and jumped in, crouching low.

My prisoner was in the room, still cuffed to the log box. He did not move and there was no sign of anyone else in the room. I kept my gun at the ready and searched the cottage, bedrooms, closets, everything. There was nobody there but me and the prisoner, who still had not moved. I put my gun away and went to look at him.

His head was turned away from me, lying with one cheek on the stones surrounding the stove. I didn't like the look of him. He was too still. Had I hurt him more badly than I thought?

Still wary, I crouched and knelt on his free hand, then rolled his face toward me. He was dead, but it was nothing I had done. Someone had battered him with a log from the box. He had a massive injury over one eye and a second wound, a depression in the region of the temple. Blood had seeped out and matted, drying on the stones and sticking his hair to the surface.

I checked for a pulse automatically, even though I've seen enough corpses to know that this battler had thrown his last karate chop.

11

I did the only thing that made any sense—unlocked my handcuffs and put them back in their pouch. There was nothing to be done for the dead man, this side of an inquest, anyway. I had nothing to gain from staying here. I pulled the curtains over the window in case there was a sniper out there waiting for a clear shot at me. It didn't seem likely. They would not have drawn a bead. They would have thrown another grenade through the window once I was inside. If they had any more. But I was nervous and I did the only thing I could to protect myself.

There was a telephone on the kitchen wall. Not surprisingly, most of our island cottages are owned by wealthy people. They can afford the luxury of a phone cable even when they still go along with the anachronism of oil or gas lamps. A phone line is cheap, hydro lines for adequate power cost thousands to install. I picked up the phone and dialed the emergency number of the Ontario Provincial Police.

The voice at the other end said, "Corporal Reinhardt," and I felt better at once. I knew Harry Reinhardt. He was the station officer who contacted me when there were missing kids or stolen cars that might end up in a backwater like Murphy's Harbour—routine stuff. I'd struck up enough of a phone friendship with him to have had him and his family fishing up here last fall. He was a steady guy.

"Harry, this is Reid Bennett at the Harbour."

"Hi, Reid. Hell of a night, what are you up to?"

"I'm up to my axles in trouble, is what. I've still got that kidnapping and homicide I called you about, but now I've got two more homicides to report."

"Two more?" His voice went up an octave.

"Three altogether. The strangling, a blast victim, Irv Whiteside, the guy who runs—make that used to run—the Lakeside Tavern, and now a guy who called himself Nighswander, blunt instrument."

"Jesus Christ." He took a deep breath. "What in hell's going on?"

"It would take all night to explain but it started with the kidnapping. I need some troops, and I need 'em bad."

"Listen, Reid, we've got nothing moving right now, but I'll put you through to Parry Sound. Talk to the Inspector, he's the senior man tonight."

I thanked him and waited and another voice said, "Inspector Anderson."

"Chief Bennett, Murphy's Harbour. Inspector, we've got big trouble here." I gave him the outline and he asked a few questions—good questions that made me admit I had no idea what was going on or where it was likely to end, but that it could go on some more and maybe leave us with another corpse—the Carmichael girl. I didn't add that it might leave me dead in the snow. He would think I was over-dramatizing.

He paused and I bored in. "I need your help, Inspector. I need a roadblock on the highway, north and south of the turn-off to the Harbour. And I'd like a check of motels for a vehicle towing an empty snowmobile trailer. It might give me a lead on the people involved."

He snorted an officious little laugh. "So you need help.

You're into something you can't solve with a gun and you come crawling to the proper authorities."

"I'm not crawling, I'm following authorized procedures." I could guess what he was going to say and I wanted it over so we could go back to being two policemen on parallel courses instead of haughty parent and delinquent child—me.

"Authorized procedures are for me to be responsible for my own region, not for some Wild West war hero who stirs up a mess and then comes running."

"Let's skip the editorials. I'm doing the same as you—my best. I've been chasing down the disappearance of a girl. Now it's gone beyond one man's ability to handle and I'm asking for expanded help."

"Just like you did last summer, when we had to come up and bail you out."

That finally made me mad. "You couldn't bail out a leaky punt. Your men arrived in time to find me with all the troublemakers laid out like cordwood. All they did was get their names in the goddamn paper."

"That's it." He was gleeful now. "That's what you're after, publicity, glamor. You're not a policeman, you're a goddamn amateur."

"Cut the crap." It is not the way to speak to OPP inspectors, but he was way off limits. "I've carried out my duties here to the limit of my abilities. Now I'm asking you for the extended care you're paid to provide. Are you going to do it or not?"

"Who the hell do you think you're talking to?"

I had never met Inspector Anderson, but I could imagine him at the other end, veins swelling in his neck above the clean white collar he hadn't had to soil by climbing cabins and fighting with potential killers. I could see his clerk, some OPP constable, looking on respectfully while he thundered.

"I think I'm talking to a professional peace officer who has sworn the same oath as I have to uphold the same laws and to assist other police departments as requested. Is that true or isn't it?"

That got through. It was all kosher. Once the murderer left my patch he was the target of all policemen. It was this man's duty to help me, no matter how much he resented the publicity I'd gotten the year before for sorting out a problem singlehanded.

After a long pause he came back more calmly, still not apologetic. "If you stop and look out of the window, you will observe that it's snowing."

"I'm at a homicide scene on an island. I arrived here five minutes back by snowmobile."

That silenced him completely, and he went on more reasonably when he began again. "Then you should appreciate that the highways are closed. Nothing's moving. I've got three cars out and they're all snowed in at gas stations. The snowplow driver has been pulled off the road for the night. He'll start again when it stops coming down."

That much was good news. It meant we were sealed off from the rest of the world. The only way out was by skidoo, and even that wasn't certain. The kidnappers wouldn't move the girl far tonight. By daylight, when the roads opened again, it would be different. A fresh inspector would be on duty with the OPP and he would do what I needed, instigate a search of all cars leaving our area.

The Inspector cut into my planning. "Are you still there? I said the snowplow is off the road."

"Thank you for your information. I'll call back at daylight." I hung up and rang Harry Reinhardt back to talk police work.

"Harry, Reid again. I heard about the highway. I figure my rounders were heading for Toronto, but they'll have to wait. Can you do some phoning for me?"

He could and would. With nobody on the road he had no

radio work to carry out, and all the law-abiding people of the region had been in bed for hours. He was glad of something to do.

"Fine. I need a check of the motels within a few miles each side of us, maybe the first dozen each way. Have they had any arrivals since eleven or so. If they have, descriptions. If you make a note for me, I'll call later and chase down any likely ones as soon as the plow's been through."

With all that accomplished I turned out the gas light and left the way I had entered. I made a point of jumping out of the door, but nobody shot at me so I clipped on my snow-shoes and went back through the never-ending snow to my skidoo. I was glad to feel that the wind was dropping and the weather seemed a fraction less savage.

The machine started first pop and I headed back, keeping well north of the crack in the ice I had seen earlier, checking all the time to my right to be sure I wasn't closing on it. I was very anxious about Nancy Carmichael but I decided I would hit the mainland where I could and head back to the station, hang my little trailer behind the skidoo, and bring Sam with me for support. I would carry the station shotgun and head back to check all the cottages on this side of the lake. When I saw any signs of people coming and going, I would storm in. No law-abiding soul would have gone further than his woodpile tonight. Movement would mean intruders, which might mean Nancy and her gang.

These people must have thought they were clever, lifting her in Murphy's Harbour, but now they were locked in until the snow let up and I planned to use that time to nail them.

A ridge loomed in the ice ahead. I should have gotten off and tapped around it, making sure it was safe. But tired and preoccupied like I was, I didn't. Instead I opened the machine full bore and went over it.

I was twelve inches off the snow when the bullet zinged off the metal at the front of the machine.

My military self took over. I pushed the machine to the right and rolled off to the left. The ice was hard and I rolled three times before stopping, coming up with my gun in my hand. I lay for a second staring ahead through the snow and the darkness until I saw the muzzle flash of a gun.

It was forty yards ahead of me—about twenty from the skidoo, which had stopped when I released the throttle. That's a lunatic range for a handgun even if you can see the target clearly, which I couldn't. I ran forward, stopping every five steps to roll down and sideways, first left, then right. There were no more shots and I was halfway to the place where I had seen the flash. I stayed low, my gun pointed at the place. I saw the muzzle flash again, an oval blast of flame that let me know he was aiming at the machine, three-quarters of the right angle away from me. I knelt and fired, two handed. My gun only clicked. I fired again. Another click. That had never happened to me before with any weapon. I was lucky this wasn't any of the ambushes I'd encountered in Nam, otherwise some medic would be stuffing me into a body bag a minute or two from now.

I pulled the trigger a third time. Nothing. And as I realized that the girl on the ice must have emptied the gun, I saw a jet of sparks from the exhaust of a snow machine. The ambusher was getting away. Groping in my pants pocket for my spare shells, I ran after him, opening the chamber of the Colt as I ran, thumbing in a couple of bullets and snapping it shut. Before I could stop to aim, the sparks were snuffed out. I stopped and swore, then kept walking, gun held at the ready. And then I heard the cry. It was a man, terrified, drowning. His machine had gone into the cut.

I moved on slowly, pushing my gun back in my pocket. Through the teeth of the snow that needled my eyes I could see the black split in the ice surface. That was all, but I could hear the whimpering cry of a man in his last moments. I lay flat on the ice and squirmed forward toward the crack. With my weight spread, I should be safe enough to pull him out. And I wanted him. I wanted him badly. I shouted, "Over here. Kick! Kick!" and he spluttered something that I couldn't make out. He was five feet from me, buoyed up by the fancy down parka he was wearing, but by the look of him he couldn't swim. I knelt and took off my parka. The ice creaked under me and I dropped flat at once. I took out the gun and slipped it into the waistband of my pants, then flicked out the end of the parka to him. He grabbed it and pulled himself to the edge of the ice. I let him come, then, as he was trying to grip the ice surface, I whisked the parka away from him and he yelled again—a terrified squeal like a stuck pig.

I edged forward another foot or two until we were at arm's length. He stuck his hand out to me frantically but I didn't take it. "Where's the woman?"

He couldn't answer anything so complex, could hardly speak. "Please. I can't swim in these clothes. Help me." He made a weak attempt to pull himself up but I said nothing, just pulled on my parka, grateful that only the outside had gotten wet.

"You'll freeze and sink in about one more minute," I told him, and he screamed again, a choked, breathless wail of panic.

I knelt, and he held out one hand again but I still didn't take it. "Where are they keeping the woman? Tell me or I'll walk away and leave you."

"In a cottage near here. Get me out and I'll take you there, honestly." He was stuttering with cold. A few more seconds and he would be too far gone to help himself. A tougher, calmer man might have lasted five minutes. He was too weak and scared. He would die.

"Which cottage?"

His face was a white disk, like a cartoonist's impression. The eyes and mouth were dark circles. Without help he would die soon and I was tempted to leave him, but he came through with an answer.

"On the point. Please. I'll take you there."

Now I reached out and took his hand, taking care to hold him by the fingers. I didn't want him gripping me and sliding me along the ice into the water beside him. "Kick hard and pull your belly up on the ice," I shouted. And when he made no move I shook his hand, snapping the words up into his brain. "Kick hard and lift your belly on top."

He did it, half clearing the water, and I was able to tug him back. The ice edge crumbled under him and he whimpered with fear, but I held on and he finally slithered out, flat on the surface, wet and black as a seal, gasping and spitting water.

I dragged him back well clear of the cut, and pulled him to his feet. He was tall, big enough to be trouble when he dried out, and I still had to move him with me on my snow machine. Because he had already tried to kill me and might do so again I did what I had to, clinically. As he stood staring at me, teeth chattering, I drew my stick and chopped him hard on the brachial plexus of his right arm. He yelped and held the place with his left hand, but his right hung limp. He would not be a threat for an hour or two.

"Try anything funny and I'll immobilize your other arm." I meant it. He was getting off lightly. "Now run." I shoved him and he turned and started stumbling over the ice, holding his dead right arm in his left hand, toward the light of my snow machine.

I ambled after him and reached the machine before he did. He got on behind me, holding timidly with his left hand onto my shoulder. I started away, trying to recreate the map of the lake in my mind. The point he meant was north of us on the clear ice, north of the cut, about a quarter of a mile away. By the time we got there his clothes would be an icy suit of armor and he would be close to frostbite or pneumonia. I had to move fast.

104

I gunned away, keeping straight and careful so he could hold on. His teeth were chattering just behind my ear and he was making a small whimpering sound like a spanked child. I didn't expect any trouble from him.

I followed parallel to the crack in the ice all the way to the shore line, realizing that they had known I must do so and had set up the ambush accordingly. I wondered if they had a second layer of defense. They hadn't, and I turned left, heading north. "Point the place out," I shouted over my shoulder.

After a minute or so he started shaking my shoulder, then swayed nervously as he let go with his left hand to point awkwardly around me. "Over there. Look." It was a two-story place set close to the water. There were lights in the downstairs windows. That meant they were not expecting me. They were waiting for their boy to come back with the news that he had wasted me so they could all raise their glasses and toast the revolution. Then they would come out and tie my body to my snow machine and push it through the ice. I would never be found. The perfect crime. Except that I had survived and was here, ready to shoot anybody who tried to finish what my prisoner had started.

I decided on boldness. They would be expecting their own man to come back, lights blazing. As far as they were concerned, this was his machine. I slowed, then stopped to pull out my gun and reload all the chambers. I would have words for the woman in my second cell when I got back to the station.

With the gun loaded I pulled off my right glove and gripped the Colt properly. Then I told the prisoner, "Get off. Walk in front and don't do anything to let them know I'm with you. If you do, I bust your head."

He was so rigid with cold that he could barely get off the machine and his teeth were chattering too hard for him to speak. I jabbed him with the gun, hard. I wanted him terrified of me. I didn't know how many people were inside or how well they were armed. If I could cancel him, out of fear, it was one less variable to worry about.

He started up the steps from the dock, bent over like an old man with the rigidity that had set in during our short ride. Nobody had noticed our arrival. Or if they had, they hadn't put on any outside lights. He stumbled and I prodded him again, in the kidney. He was too cold to feel much but he moaned and tried to move faster up the steps. I saw there was only one skidoo outside the door. It had been driven right up the rock that sloped out of the lake. It had been parked in the lee of the building and was almost free of new snow. I wondered where the other machine could be, and what its absence meant in future trouble.

As we reached the door I prodded my guy one last time and growled at him, "Open it up and say nothing. Understand?"

He nodded, a tight, tuning-fork tremor of his head. We passed in front of the window, me crouched as low as I could, out of the line of sight. He reached the front door and fumbled with it, his frozen left hand hardly able to press the latch.

He opened it, and then the inner door, and I was struck with the sudden, ridiculously fragrant aroma of hot coffee. He stepped into the room, the big main living room of the cottage, and I shoved him aside, tripping him so he sprawled helplessly on the rug, and swept the room with a glance. There were two women sitting there but neither one was Nancy Carmichael, and I swore. These were not the women I wanted. I wanted Nancy.

12

W here's the girl?" I shouted it and they shrank back, open mouthed with fear and surprise. "The girl, Carmichael. Where is she?"

The older one spoke then. She was perhaps fifty-five, and I recognized her as the duck hunter I had seen months earlier at her own place on Frog Island. She was short and growing heavier with middle age but she had an olive complexion and a patrician look that would have commanded respect anywhere, even among people who knew she was full-blooded Ojibway and not a Roman countess.

"I don't know. She went with the man," she said. She was shaken. They had obviously expected me to be out of their lives for keeps. Now here I was, risen from the dead, waving a gun and spoiling their plans. And I was angry enough to shake anybody.

"Who else is in this cottage, besides you people?" I kept my gun on them and the younger one looked first at her partner, then at me, wondering where to find direction. She was trembling, while the older woman had become calm again. It was the older one who said finally, "There's nobody here. Do you want to search the place?"

"Yes. You come with me. You others lie on the floor and put your hands on top of your heads. Face down. Do it!"

The man I had brought in was glad to be where there was warmth. He squirmed close to the stove and lay there in a cloud of steam, his bare hands stretched out to the heat. I should have warned him they would be agonizing when they thawed out but he didn't care, not yet.

The younger woman knelt, then flattened herself as I had said. I turned to the older woman. "Go in front of me and don't get cute. There's three people dead already. I don't mind making it four."

"We're alone here," she said. I could tell from the vibrato in her voice that she was scared, but she did not show it in any other way. She was a tough lady.

"Lead the way. Open each door in turn and take two steps inside." She went ahead of me, first into the kitchen and the bathroom on the ground floor, then upstairs to each of the three bedrooms. I looked under all the beds, in the closets. There was nobody there. As we started down the stairs I could see that the two people in the living room were lying the way I had ordered them to, so I pushed my gun back into the holster pocket. "Draw all the drapes," I told the woman. She did. "Right. Now you get down on the floor like the others."

She did and I walked into the bathroom and pulled out all the towels I could see. I threw them to the man. "Here. Strip and dry yourself." He reached up and caught them clumsily with his left hand. I studied him more closely. He was young, perhaps twenty-three. He had blonde hair a little too long, an intellectual's cut. He was lean but not hard, a man who watched every mouthful he ate but never exercised. He stood up and stripped, still shivering. He made no attempt to conceal his nakedness from the women and it confirmed what I was beginning to think. He was not interested in them. Women were nonpersons. I saw that he had a good tan except for a bikini-sized patch at his loins. He was well-off. January tans are rare in Murphy's Harbour, except for the brown, burned faces of the bush-workers. Jamaica isn't on our circuit. And he had a petulant look about him, a droop to the corners of his mouth. I didn't like anything about him.

But I did the charitable thing anyway. The coffee pot was on the propane stove in the kitchen. I poured two cups and returned to give him one. He took it and sipped noisily, spilling coffee down his bare chest and onto the towel he had finally wrapped around him. I sipped my own, then set it on the table. It was strong and I could feel the effect of the caffeine at once, like a jolt behind my eyes.

I undid my parka, noticing almost with surprise that it was wet from my rescue work, took the gun from the pocket, and slipped out of the parka and hung it over a chair back close to the stove.

"You can sit up now," I told the women. "Crossed-legged, hands on your heads."

They turned over and rolled themselves up, sitting as I told them. The younger one had gotten her own courage back now and she said, "Really, is all this play-acting necessary?"

I kept my voice reasonable but let the anger come through in my expression. "So far, since this kidnapping happened, one of your party has been strangled. A man has been killed with a hand grenade and another man has been beaten to death. You will do as I say or I will take whatever action I deem necessary. Understood?"

She looked at the older woman. "Somebody's dead? Freddie didn't make it?"

"Strangled. And it's not Freddie. She's in custody. It's the woman in cabin six at the motel. Her name was Katie."

I was watching the older woman. You learn to read faces, to pick out genuine reactions from carefully rehearsed responses. Her shock was genuine. Her mouth fell open. The killing was news to her.

The young man was still standing, hunching his back as he pushed himself close to the stove for warmth. I gestured to him. "You sit down, like the others." He did it, moving languidly. His circle might have found it coquettish. He tucked his towel around his front and lowered himself gracefully. He had thawed through and could be trouble.

"You three are going to prison," I told them. "Your little game of hide-and-seek has been infiltrated by real criminals. The best deal you can hope for will come from working with me before anybody else gets hurt." None of them spoke. The older woman looked at me impassively, the boy made a big show of yawning. Only the younger woman looked concerned. I concentrated on her.

"Where have you put Nancy Carmichael? Why isn't she here?"

I studied her face. It was pinched and pale, the complexion of late nights and black coffee and too many cigarettes. Whoever she was, there was nothing joyful in her life. The ideal member for a team like this. But she was slowly getting control of her fears and she did not rush to tell me what I wanted to know. At last it was the other woman who spoke, in a flat hostile voice. "She was supposed to go to my place on the island. When we got there that loud-mouth from the Tavern at the dock in town was there. He'd broken in. He said Nancy had hired him as a bodyguard. Nancy said she hadn't made any such request. So we left him there, sabotaged his machine, and went on."

It wasn't the story Irv had told but there was no way to check it. "Went on where? I already know about the island."

She moved a strand of iron-gray hair away from her eyes, looking oddly young as she did so—a grade-school girl in a wig. I was aware that she had once been beautiful, the kind of peach you find occasionally in out-of-the-way places, like villes I have seen in Nam and Indian reserves.

"We came here. This is our fall-back rendezvous."

"So where's the Carmichael girl? And where's the big heavy guy who went with you to Carl Simmonds's place?"

"They went on."

"Where?" I almost shouted it. "You're dealing with murder here. If the kid is killed you'll die before you get out of the pen. While you've got a chance, help me."

She shrugged. "I can't tell you what I don't know." I didn't believe her. She knew, but she also knew that I wouldn't try to force her to tell. Not a woman. But I was angry enough to turn and grab the young man by the hair and pull him to his feet. His towel slipped and he tugged at it with his left hand, wincing. "Where did you get your instructions to shoot me?"

He decided to play it tough. Except for the whack on the collarbone I had done nothing to let him know I hated his guts. I'd rescued him, given him coffee. Now he was warm and secure and had seen that I hadn't pressed the women. "I have nothing to say to you," he said primly. "You're an enemy of the people."

I cracked him a baseball pitcher's swing across the mouth. It landed like a gunshot and sent him cartwheeling to the corner of the room in a tangle of arms and legs. I went over to him and prodded him with my foot. He looked up, wide-eyed in horror. Nobody had ever explained things to him quite that simply before.

I crouched and spoke to him in a soft tone, the way you talk to mean horses. "We can do this one of three ways," I explained. "You can tell me what you know right now. Or we can take your towel away and sit you out in a snowdrift until you feel like talking. Or I can save time by sitting you on the stove."

He stared at me through honestly terrified eyes. This was the first time he had seen the real face of violence. Up until now it had been a game, as intellectual as chess. Good guys versus bad guys. See the good guys make a bomb. See the

111

bad guys lose. Point made, no harm done—not to the good guys. Now he understood Bennett's Axiom, a rule I had been taught on two continents. Pain hurts.

"I'll talk," he said shakily. And then he added the most surprising comment I had heard all night. "You don't have to torture me. This isn't Viet Nam."

I looked into his eyes but there was no sarcasm there, just fear. "How did you know I was in Viet Nam?"

He waved his working hand, dismissing the question. "We checked this town out from top to bottom before we decided to join in."

"Who's we?"

He straightened up, imperious, except for the purple and white clown stripes on his left cheek. "The People's Revolutionary Guard."

"Is C.L.A.W. some part of the same outfit?" Know your enemy, even if he uses dumb names to throw you off.

He laughed, a condescending, bitter sound. "C.L.A.W. is just a bunch of brainless broads playing games."

The younger woman shouted something. I told her, "Shut up. You can have your turn in a minute." She subsided and I bored in on the kid.

"How many of your Guard are up here tonight?" It was the least he could tell me. I wanted more, names, locations—especially locations—but numbers would be a start.

"Four."

"Names?" I took out my notebook, then realized I had gutted it to start a fire in the fishing hut a thousand years earlier. I looked around for paper and found a writing pad tucked into the top drawer of a sideboard against the wall. "Names?" I asked again, and he began to back off.

"I took an oath."

"Yeah, so did I, but mine is for the greatest happiness of the greatest number, so forget yours."

"I can't break it," he said unsteadily.

"If you don't, somebody else is liable to get hurt and the first candidate would be you," I said softly.

He backed away, a pace closer to the stove and the reminder of my threat.

"You heard him." He appealed to the women. "This policeman threatened to torture me. He said he would sit me on the stove. I have to talk."

The older woman surprised me. "Why talk? Say nothing, you scum. I'd like to see you burn."

That ended any play-acting on his part. He gave me the names. His own was Elliot. Really it was Peter Hawthorne, but he had always admired T.S. Eliot so he had taken the name as his code name. Eliot was an English poet, he explained helpfully. I didn't bother explaining that I had read the occasional book. The others were Michael and Sam and Tom. Tom was the leader, the heavy-set mystery man who had trashed Carl Simmonds's house.

"Is that his last name, or what?"

"First name, of course." He was surprised. He had never visited an Indian reserve where half the men had surnames that had once been somebody's Christian name.

"Where was he when he asked you to wait for me on the ice and shoot down my headlights?"

"At our field headquarters." He was enjoying talking now. He had slowed his delivery, like the drunk who gets you in a corner and holds you by the lapel.

"Don't play games. Where were you geographically, not philosophically?"

"It was the cottage on the island." Now he hesitated, looking up at me as if measuring the odds of my hitting him again. He needn't have worried. Hitting isn't a hobby with me. It's an occasional function I have to attend to, but I don't enjoy it. He looked down at the floor and mumbled, "We were at the cottage where you killed Michael."

More gasping from the women. I ignored them. "Did you

arrive at the same time as Tom? And if so, was the man dead when you got there?"

"Tom was there before me. He was examining Michael. Michael's head was a *mess!*" From the way his voice ran up at the end of the sentence he might have been describing a bad haircut rather than a fatal beating.

"Was the Carmichael girl with Tom?"

"No." He shook his head. His hair had dried completely now and I could see that it was dark at the roots.

"And where had you come from?"

He had come from another motel, just south of the park. He had driven his vehicle there after dropping the women off, and had picked up a skidoo from there. He had gone to the cottage on the island, found Tom, listened to the tale of my villainy, and had waited close to the cut to ambush me and revenge his group. He had waited for the first skidoo. Tom had told him it would be me, that I was too dangerous to tackle in a fair fight, I would have to be taken by surprise.

"Where are the others—Tom and what's his name, Sam?" I asked the one question but I needed answers to twenty. The second one would have been, Why had the three men shown themselves at the Lakeshore Tavern? Why give anybody a clear look at you when you plan to be involved in a crime? The only answer that made sense was vanity. They had enjoyed the limelight of fighting in the bar, never guessing that they would be seen again later. They hadn't expected any real resistance. I wondered if one of them was staked out for me close to the station, waiting for me to come back, waiting with another gun—perhaps a shotgun this time—something that would put me away for keeps.

"I don't know." He shrugged his shoulders, though one of them didn't work. His towel slipped and he gripped it with his good hand.

I pushed him some more, went over the questions again, but nothing new came out. He was scared enough to be telling the truth. Which meant the girl was still missing and that there were two people somewhere outside this cabin who could justify themselves if they killed me.

Neither of the women added anything to what he had told me. Under steady questioning, the younger one said that it must have been Nancy's blabbing that let the People's Revolutionary Guard know what was going to happen. But she herself knew nothing about the Guard. If it was a terrorist group, it was new.

So far in Canada we've been lucky. The only terrorists we've had have been the Quebec F.L.Q., a bunch of Moscow-sponsored hooligans who stirred up the country for a few months during 1970. Our federal government gets all its strength in Quebec and most of the bad boys had been allowed to get away with their murder. They had been given free passage to Cuba, whence they went on to France and came home after ten years to the kind of jail terms you expect for stealing candies. In the meantime, the Royal Canadian Mounted Police, who had been told to prosecute them, had themselves been arrested and hassled. I guess we don't have terrorists because the other side doesn't have much more to win here.

I gave up and concentrated on the older woman. "You must be 'Margaret.' What's your last name?"

"Sumner." That meant she would be Mrs. I've never met a Sumner on any of the Indian reserves. We have lots of Sinclair's, no Sumners.

"Mrs. Sumner. You understand that this Tom character has killed two men—one with a booby trap, the other one beaten to death. He may also be the person responsible for killing your own group member under the name of Katie at the motel."

"All this is assumption," she said quietly.

"I also know that you and he wrecked Carl Simmonds's house."

115

She looked away from me, gazing at the stove as if it were a Rodin sculpture. Her profile was toward me and I could see how she had impressed these younger women. There was strength and dignity to her that looked classical.

"I'm not proud of what we did. I just wanted those negatives."

"That's a great comfort to him as he cleans up the damage."

"I'll pay." She glared at me, nostrils pinched. "I'll compensate the little faggot, don't worry."

That surprised me. It was the first heat she had shown. Was she herself a fag-basher? Most women aren't, only insecure men need to thump homosexuals, but there was real hatred in her voice. No, the wild card in the deck was Tom. I turned the topic back to him.

"I need to know where Tom has taken the girl. She's in real danger."

She said nothing and I tried a new tack. "He has already killed, and he nearly killed another one of your group, that girl he stripped on the ice and left to die." That was when Mrs. Sumner laughed at me, a big, genuine laugh right down to her gut, shaking her whole body, making her let go of her head and dangle her arms helplessly.

"You predictable, chauvinist bastard. Don't you understand? He didn't strip her. She volunteered."

13

My astonishment opened her up like a book. She couldn't tell me fast enough what a fool I'd been. They had seen me overtaking them across the ice, my headlight bobbing along behind. Margaret had been in front and she had stopped close to the fishing huts and made her suggestion to the girl. The plan was for them to leave her where they were sure I would find her, then press on with the lights out, Margaret in the lead. I guess she had the knack of finding her way in the dark better than most people can follow street signs. They would have their lights out, although she had bet that I wouldn't come after them even if I saw their lights, not with a damsel in distress to rescue.

So I had done my Sir Galahad impersonation and they had gotten away and Irv Whiteside was dead. The girl had done her own part by unloading my gun when I left it with her so I would be at a disadvantage next time I needed it.

The two women and the kid in his towel all had a good smirk at my predictability, but I ignored them. If people can still get my attention by expecting me to act humanely, I have nothing to be ashamed of.

When they had made their point, I acted a little humble. It worked. Margaret gave me her version of the story. She was serious about feminist action. They had planned this kidnapping as a rehearsal. They knew about my service in Viet Nam, but with the feminine equivalent of arrogance they had ignored it as a threat. To them it made me some kind of knee-jerk trigger-puller with no brains. I was obviously no match for a subtle group of women. The only fly in their ointment was Nancy's failure to understand she was just the cheese in a mousetrap, not the star of the show. She had bragged about the plan to some boy and he had let it slip to somebody else, and finally a member of this crazy Guard group had heard and wanted in. It would give them some cheap and easy publicity. And even more important, it would give them leverage in their struggle against the arms race. As I already knew, Nancy's father was the president of Astro-Control Systems, the Toronto outfit that made guidance systems for American missiles. Some wild-eyed group had already bombed the plant. Now this new outfit was planning to do by stealth what the others had failed to do with dynamite.

At least that was my guess, and it made me sure that the Carmichael kid was dead if I didn't get her back tonight.

I asked how C.L.A.W. had reacted to the news that Nancy had done everything to blow security short of writing an editorial for the college paper. Apparently like all democratically run lunatic fringes they had taken a vote and decided to proceed. They had counted on the Guard group to give them what Margaret described cryptically as "firepower."

The dead girl at the highway had struck up a romance with one of the Guard people, I couldn't find out which one, and that had intensified the complications.

"Doesn't it bother you that this Katie is dead? And the same guys who killed her now have another member, young Nancy? Don't you care?"

Margaret Sumner looked at me with something like amusement. "No," she said.

118

The other girl protested. "We don't want anybody harmed, we're a peaceful group." But Margaret Sumner had the last word.

"We don't care," she said.

I gave up and asked the last, hopeless question. "Why did you set this particular heist up? What have you got against Carmichael that you'd put his daughter in this kind of danger?"

She looked at me impassively, the true believer talking to the heretic. "You don't need to know. It's personal."

I gave up. None of them knew enough about this Tom character to suit me. He was the wild card in the deck, unknown even to the kid who had fired at me. I wondered what kind of zealot he was. These Guard groups spring up from time to time, mostly made up of spoiled rich kids doing something about their Oedipus complexes by opposing the church or corporate profits, anything, right or wrong, with more seniority than they've got. Mostly they just march and sing. They're harmless and their members grow up to be teachers and newspaper columnists who vote Socialist.

But this man sounded different. Elliot's description of him was the key. He had described him as "around thirty-five." By that age he should have shucked his activism along with his acne. I was worried, but too tired and stretched to know what to do about it.

In the end I left them all there. There was no way to take them back in. If I put them on another skidoo in front of mine they could break for it. I didn't want to waste time chasing them down. It was even too much of a problem to bring in Elliot, so I handcuffed him and left him nude except for his towel. It would prevent his getting dressed, which meant he wouldn't be bothering me before the weather warmed up. I'd be back by then. In the meantime I would be free to chase down the skidoo tracks that led away from here.

I considered tying up the women, but instead immobilized them by taking all their outdoor clothing and the plug lead from the snowmobile outside. I also tore the phone out of the wall. It was primitive and illegal but I had no choice. Two men who had killed before were outside somewhere, waiting for me. I didn't want them to be reinforced or even warned from here.

I took the outdoor clothes with me out to my snow machine, which was covered with snow by now. Fortunately it started easily, and I headed out behind the cabin onto the roadway. It was drifted in and I had to curtsey around the edges of the worst drifts, but I could see the track of another machine ahead of me. I followed it, pulling my face down into my collar, longing for a chance to curl up in a corner out of the snow and sleep like a dog.

The bite of the snowflakes that fluttered around the windshield kept me from dozing. I drove along the stale track up to the edge of Murphy's Harbour proper, around the curve that matches the curve of the bay, past the bait store and past the point where the track turned off, toward the side door of the Lakeside Tavern.

I was wide awake now, but I didn't pull in. Instead I did the clever thing, winding up the throttle and passing the place at a roar, heading up and over the hump beside the bridge above the lock and around the first corner toward the police station.

That's where I stopped, slipped on my snowshoes, and tramped back, keeping off the center of the road although the light on the bridge was so obscured by flying snow that nobody could have seen me from the Tavern. The side door was locked, but this is a small town. Irv Whiteside once showed me where he kept the key, in a coffee can under one of the beams that supports the side of the Tavern on pilings over the water. I think he left it there in case any friends want liquor. They took what they wanted and paid him on Monday when he opened again. That way he wasn't bootlegging—they were breaking in.

I took the key and opened the side door, very softly. My snowshoes were propped outside in a drift. It's an old building and it creaks in the wind. I hoped the wind would cover the sound of my entrance. There is another door sealing off the inside so that my entrance wouldn't be announced by a blast of cold snowy air.

I went up the stairs. I knew Irv had a couple of rooms he rented, two he used for himself. I tried his room first. It was locked, of course, but the simple Yale slipped in a moment to my knife blade. I squatted low to the floor and shone my flashlight around. The room was neat. There was a TV set and some comfortable furniture, including a double bed, but nothing more. The adjacent room was filled with stores, mostly liquor. I went back out, locking the door again.

The next door was also locked and I went through the same procedure. A quick search showed it was the room occupied by Nancy's parents. It was empty except for their clothes and toiletries.

As I touched the third door I heard a low sound inside, muffled, half scream, half burble. It made the hair prickle on the back of my neck. It sounded as if someone had a woman held hostage, one hand over her mouth, the other very probably holding a gun that would be pointed at the door. I stood to one side of the door frame as I slipped the lock with my left hand, eased the door open with my right. When I had it open a millimeter past the catch point I drew my gun and hurled myself inside, rolling away from the door as I landed. I collided with the end of the bed, but not hard enough to bother me. I lay perfectly still for a half second. The sound persisted but there was no scuffling of feet, nothing to indicate a struggle, only the squeaking and rocking of the bedstead against my shoulder.

I crouched, moving a pace to the left and holding my flashlight over my head at what must have looked like chest height. Nobody fired at me. I flashed it over the bed. In the beam I saw the shifting pattern on the bed, white flesh and black shadows writhing like snakes. I scuttled around the bed and into the bathroom. There was nobody there. Only then did I come back into the bedroom, still wary, and switch on the light.

Nancy Carmichael was tied to the wooden bedstead. She was naked and spread-eagled, her ankles and wrists tied to the corners. She had a scarf around her head, the folded thickness of it jammed into her open mouth. Her eyes were rolled toward me like those of a frightened horse. I went to the bed and patted her ankle. "I'll be back, I have to search the place."

She moaned again. I could read the anguish but I had to be sure there was nobody downstairs, and I believed there was. There had been no tracks away from the building.

I turned off the light so I wouldn't be silhouetted, then advanced, gun drawn, to the head of the stairs. I was crouching automatically, as I've crouched a thousand times in enemy areas.

It saved my life again. As I reached the top of the stairs a bullet came out of the darkness, an inch high over my head instead of through my throat. I fired at once down the muzzle flash, then again, lower, not even stopping to think.

I heard the rushing collapse of a falling body and the clatter of a dropped gun. I fell to the floor and held my light above me, shining it down the stairs.

The first thing I saw were feet. Then the foreshortened length of a man's body lying head down on the staircase. I could see nothing moving beyond. It didn't mean he was alone. I stood up, still crouching carefully, and ran down the stairs. There was a handgun, some kind of automatic, lying beside the body. I booted it away but did not stop until I was through the doorway at the bottom and had rolled sideways against the bar.

I crouched, listening. The only sound was the creaking of the building under the northeast wind and the sand-storm rustle of the tiny brittle snowflakes against the windows. I switched on my flashlight and flicked it over the room. It seemed empty. Moving carefully, I went back to the doorway and found the light switch.

The lights fluttered for a moment, then settled down, and I could see that the place was empty. Gun in hand, I searched the rest of the lower level. It was deserted. There was a bottle on the counter and a half-filled glass. I looked at it in disbelief. My gunman had been relaxing over a glass of Bailey's Irish Cream. Jesus! They don't make hoodlums like they used to. He was trained enough or scared enough to keep the lights off so nobody could see him in the bar. Perhaps he had been expecting me. Well. Now we'd met.

I went back to him, first switching on the stairway light. He was lying as I had left him. One bullet had caught him through the chest. That must have been my first shot at the muzzle flash. The second had hit him in the left eye. He had no pulse in his throat. I had closed off any chance of getting information from him, even though he might have been as useless as Elliot back at the other cottage with the C.L.A.W. women.

I picked up his handgun. It was a Walther P.38. I slipped it into my pocket and went back to Nancy's room. As I entered and switched on the light she squirmed with fear, then relaxed as she recognized me. I took out my pocket knife and cut the scarf from her mouth. Words poured out of her instantly. "Did you shoot him? Did you?"

"He's dead, Nancy." I cut the two belts that held her wrists to the bedposts, then the stockings that tied her ankles. She sat up, sobbing. "It was awful. Gross."

"Did he molest you sexually?"

She put her hands over her pretty mouth, pressing her lips against her teeth, speaking through clenched fingers.

"He raped me. He made me . . . do things. It was terrible."
She ran out of words and sobbed helplessly.

"Come to the bathroom." I handed her a blanket and she
stumbled to her feet and came with me, tugging the blanket
around her shoulders. I took a handful of tissues from the
dispenser. "Wipe your mouth out with these." She did it,
not looking at me, not knowing what I was doing, then
hunched over the sink and vomited dry bile. I handed her a
bottle of Scope. "Use this." While she was busy I folded
the tissues she had given me and put them in my tunic
pocket. Her blanket had slipped but she did not care. I
wasn't a man. I was an act of God, blind as the snowstorm
that raged around the Tavern, keeping me from driving
her fifty miles to the nearest hospital and the help she
needed.

When she had gargled and spat a couple of times she
straightened up and looked at me. I told her, "It's important
that you wipe yourself inside and save the tissues. Can you
do that for me?"

She looked at me blankly, not replying, but I handed her
more tissues, then closed the door and waited. I had never
felt so inadequate in all my life. She needed a doctor to
check her, a woman to comfort her. I was neither. I was a
rough-and-ready copper trying to compensate for the crime
and the criminal ugliness of the weather.

I looked around the room for something to put the swabs
into. Without going through her luggage there was nothing
obvious. I called through the door, "Save the swab. I'm
going downstairs," and I went down, stepping over the body
without looking down at it.

I searched the place again from end to end to make sure
there was nobody hiding in a beer cooler or behind empty
crates. When I was sure, I went to the bar and took down
the Black Velvet. It had never tasted better. The purity of
the taste thrilled me and it went down like soft fire, spread-

124

ing out through my whole body. Then I picked up some foil wrap from the kitchen and went back up.

She answered nervously when I knocked. "Who is it?"

"Chief Bennett."

She opened the door for me and stood back, not speaking. She was wearing the bottom half of a brown pants suit and a white brassiere. I said, "I'll wait outside while you dress," but she shook her head silently so I picked up the swab she had left on the dresser and wrapped it in some of the foil. Then I took out the other and wrapped it. The move was probably unnecessary. The guy on the stairs was most likely the culprit. But if he weren't, we would need this evidence when I brought the guy in, and I intended to. Rape is the worst crime in the book, for my money. I asked her, "Do you have a lipstick I can borrow?"

She looked at me in surprise, wondering if she had heard right, and I tried a tiny laugh to let her know that the world was still rotating on its axis despite what had happened to her tonight.

"Not for me—I doubt you have my shade. I just want to mark these."

She said, "Oh," in a faint voice, and looked in her purse. The lipstick was very pale but it marked on the foil. I marked the appropriate one "Oral" and put both in my breast pocket.

She was fully dressed by now, in a fawn sweater and the jacket of her pants suit. I sat down on the bed and gestured for her to take the chair. She did, and I told her what had to happen.

"You can't stay here alone. What I'm proposing is that I take you back to the station. There's a policewoman there and you'll be safe until your parents get there. I guess they're still at the dance."

She began to weep silently, only the movement of her shoulders giving away what was happening. I stood up and squeezed her shoulder. "It's all over. You're going to be okay. Tomorrow morning, soon as the snow is cleared, your folks will take you to the hospital in Sunbridge. If they prefer they can ship you right down to Toronto on one of your dad's helicopters."

She snuffled quietly and I told her, "First off, you'll need your outdoor clothes. I've got a snowmobile just up the road. It's cold outside."

She stood up automatically and looked for her boots. They were lying beside the bed. So were her other clothes—blue jeans, the Irish sweater, and her underwear. The panties were torn. I picked them up and put them in my pocket with the swabs. More evidence. She watched me without speaking. I didn't like that. She was in shock and I didn't want her going catatonic on me. I was glad Val would be waiting at the station.

"Get your coat and we'll go." Her coat was on the back of the door on a hanger. It was raccoon, but made from lush pelts sewn in a chevron pattern. It was as expensive as most mink coats but without the pretension.

"That's good. You'll be snug in that. Put a scarf over your head and we'll go."

She came out of the room and I locked it. Anyone who chose could slip the lock in a moment as I had, but it was the closest I could come to sealing the crime scene for forensic investigation later. Nancy was taller in her boots, but frail-seeming and timid. I took her by the elbow and checked her for a moment.

"Nancy, the man I shot is lying on the stairs. He can't hurt you any more, so don't be afraid. I'll take your arm. When we get to him, tell me if he was the guy who assaulted you."

She looked at me wide-eyed, as if I were speaking a foreign language. I gave her a little nod. "Come on, now, be brave." I held her elbow and walked one step ahead of her down the stairs to the body. When we reached it I asked her, "Is he the one?"

She burst into tears, nodding her head over and over, wordlessly.

"Then he got what he deserved," I said. "Come on." We negotiated the rest of the stairs and she spoke angrily through her tears, like a child who has been wrongly scolded.

"I'd never done it with anybody before. I was a virgin."

I patted her arm. "You still are. Nobody in the world knows your secret. He's dead and the bad news died with him."

It wasn't true, but it was the best thing to say even though just telling her made me feel dirty and unshaven and uncouth. I felt the old familiar disgust growing within me. I wanted this to be over. The other member of the Guard group could go to hell for all I cared. I wanted to be in the station with Val until sanity came flooding back with the morning daylight and we could turn over Tom's description to other people and go away and rediscover the fact that gentleness still exists in the world.

Outside, the snow was still whirling and Nancy gasped as the chill hit her face. Fortified with Black Velvet and adrenalin, I didn't even notice it. I picked up my snowshoes but did not put them on. Shoulder to shoulder with Nancy, I struggled through the drifted snow to my machine. I had one bare hand on the gun in my pocket, ready to shoot if anybody fired on us, but nobody did.

I started the machine and sat on it, wearily, instead of kneeling. Nancy sat behind me, hanging on tight enough to break my heart.

I took us slowly up the road to the station. It was hard to tell, with the snow that had fallen nonstop for the last six hours, but it seemed to me that there was a skidoo trail there, that the surface had been broken in the last hour or so. I wondered if somebody had talked his way out of the Legion and headed home on his skidoo. I hoped that was it. Tom was still out somewhere, a potential for trouble, and I didn't want any more. Outnumbered and outgunned I had found Nancy, and now I wanted to wait till morning before I did any more police work. I wouldn't be able to go home to bed, but I could doze at the station.

The wind had shifted and reshaped the snowdrift beside the back door of the police station, laying it longer and lower so that I was able to pull up close to the door that led to the cells. I felt uneasy. There were definite tracks here, more recent-looking than my own. I felt my heart bump a couple of times arhythmically. Maybe I was just tired. I'd been shot at three times, had someone try to frag me, and found a rape victim. My adrenalin was running like maple sap in February.

In the silence that followed my stopping the machine I heard Sam barking inside the station. That relieved me. Whatever else happened, Val was safe. Sam could bring down any man with any weapon he could hold. I tapped Nancy on the shoulder and she followed me over the last six feet to the door. Then I whistled once, a short clear note, and Sam stopped barking. The door was locked and nobody came to open it, but that made sense. I had told Val to stay inside and she was taking no chances. I fumbled for the key and opened up, stepping in first. It's not gallant but it's sense. It put me in the firing line, if any—that's what I was paid for. Nancy wasn't.

Then I stopped and looked around with my mouth hanging open in disbelief. Val was gone. Both my prisoners were locked in one cell. Sam was locked in the other.

14

I paused only a second, but in that time I could read what had happened in the expressions on the faces of the two women. The thin one from the Legion was smiling a thin, smug little smile. The other girl was close to tears. I knew then that Val was gone. I went through the obvious drills anyway, kicking open the door to the front of the station and jumping in, gun drawn, to search it. There was no one there. The teletype was clacking under its plastic cover, the gun rack still held two guns, the same empty Coke bottles stood under the counter where the public could not see. But Val was gone.

I put my gun away and came back to the cells. Nancy Carmichael had come in and was looking at the two women with a gaze that must have told them everything that had happened to her that night. They were silent. I let Sam out of the cell and fussed him and told him he was good, then I turned to the prisoners. "What happened?" The thin one said, "Find out, pig," but the other one said, "He came for her, Chief."

"Who is *he*?" I had a hundred questions, including how

had he gotten into the station without being pinned to the floor by Sam, but for now I wanted some facts.

"The others called him 'Tom,'" the pretty girl said. I remembered she was Freddie.

"Did he say where he was taking her?" I could imagine what he would do to Valerie, was perhaps already doing. She had come to this place trusting me, trusting the whole system of Canadian law to keep her as safe as she would have been in Toronto, and now she was the hostage of a hoodlum. I knew this was no revolutionary group. Terrorists don't rape, it's a bourgeois crime. They maim and kill, but they don't rape. Bikers rape. This Revolutionary Guard talk was a smokescreen. These were personal crimes being carried out and I hadn't seen it until now, when it was too late.

"Where would he have taken her, Freddie?"

She opened her mouth to answer but the thin one cut in, her voice tingling with excitement. "Somewhere you won't find her." I reached through the bars and grabbed her by the arm, pulling her against the bars, not savagely but too close for comfort. "Stay out of this, you don't know what these people are like." Then I shook her arm away and repeated my question.

Freddie said, "I don't know, Chief. He didn't say." And the thin one added her own message. "He said you had one hour and then he was going to show her a good time."

The blood roared in my ears. I took Nancy by the shoulder and led her to the cell. "You'll have to wait, Nancy. I'll call your parents in a little while. First I have to attend to this new business." She went into the cell without speaking and I locked the door. Her face was deadly white. She sat on the wooden bunk, not looking at the others. I could understand her fear but I was more concerned about Valerie's safety.

Sam was keening as if he could explain how he had been outsmarted but I had no time to find out now. I patted his head and told him "Keep" and left him while I went into

130

the front of the station and unlocked the shotgun from the rack. I knew it was loaded but I pumped the action one time to load the chamber and pushed another round into the magazine. Then I scooped a half-dozen extra shells out of the box and slipped them into my pocket. With that gun I was the equal of fifty men.

I took the time to top up the fuel in the snow machine. I didn't want to run dry a mile from my destination and waste even more time trekking up there in snowshoes. The snow was still falling, although it seemed that the wind was slackening. I was glad of that. I had some tracking to do.

The tracking was easier than I had expected. The skidoo had followed the road almost to the bridge in town, then turned east through the trees. I followed it, keeping my speed as high as I could, ducking under branches, showered with dumps of snow from those I could not miss completely. It occurred to me that they might be setting me up for an ambush. I shouldn't be barreling down a red-ball road like this. I would never have done it in Nam, but here I didn't care. I had heard enough about this Tom to believe he meant what he said. He would want to take his revenge on me by violating Valerie. The thin girl from the Legion had told him about our relationship, I could count on that. Now he would punish her for helping me, punish us both, punish the world. Unless I got there first.

A quarter-mile north of town the tracks swung back onto the lakeshore road that serviced all the cabins along the east shore, and I began to guess where he had gone—back to the cottage where I had left Elliot and the women. I patted the shotgun that lay under my knee on the saddle of the machine. I would need it now with four people against me.

The tracks turned off on top of those I had left earlier and I slammed up beside the cottage door and jumped onto the snow, clicking off the safety from my shotgun. I opened the back screen door, not even checking to see if it was wired, and fired my first round up through the glass of the back door into the ceiling above. I heard a yell of alarm from inside and I reached in and unlocked the door.

The Elliot kid was standing facing me. He had his pants on, but the cuffs had kept him from dressing further and he had a towel over his shoulders. There was no sign of anyone else.

"On the floor," I told him. He got down, but slowly, sneeringly. I knew I was in the right place. I prayed I was still in time. "Who else is here?"

He grinned even more broadly, half bowing mockingly. "Simply everybody," he said, and I heard a woman's voice shriek, "Reid! He's holding a knife on my neck."

Two sounds blended. One was a cackle from Elliot, the other was a man's voice telling me, "She's right, Bennett, put the gun down."

I kept the gun, swinging it toward the voice, which came from upstairs. "I'm putting nothing down until I see my policewoman is all right. If she isn't I'll blow your legs off." I tried to keep my voice even. I was a businessman making an offer.

"We're coming down now," the voice said. I heard the stairs creak, then saw Valerie coming toward me. I was debating whether to drop the shotgun and draw my pistol, hoping for a shot at his elbow on the arm he must be holding up to menace her throat. But he was too clever even to give me that opportunity. He was holding her hair, pulling her head back, and the knife and his arm were out of sight behind her. "He's got it in my back now," Valerie said. Her voice was high and scratchy. I could see a thin red line along her throat. He had marked her, letting her feel the sharpness of the knife. "Put the gun down," he said again from behind her.

"What if I say no?"

"Then the next thing that happens is I push this shiv into her." He let that hang before going on, "Not to kill her. I'll hit her in the neck so she'll be a basket case. You want that?" I looked at Val. She had shut her eyes and her lips were moving softly. I knew what I had to do. If she had been a policeman or another Marine in the same situation I would not have surrendered, but she was a trusting woman in a situation she could have avoided by staying at the Legion and leaving me to play copper on my own.

"All right. You win." I pointed the gun at the floor and worked the action, spilling out the shells on the floor. "There." I tossed it aside and Elliot jumped past me to grab it, then grovel for the shells, stuffing them back into the magazine.

"One's enough. Cock it and hold it on him." The man had straightened up now behind Valerie. He was dark, with an unkempt beard, but his clothes were expensive. I judged him to be five-eleven, two hundred pounds, and he looked mean. He pushed Valerie to one side and she sprawled away from him onto the couch. Then he flipped his knife, a neat little motion that made it circle once and thunk into the panel wall.

Elliot was holding the gun on me, aiming at my stomach. The other man came forward, staring at me as if I were in a zoo. He stayed clear of the gun. I had no chance to swing him in front of it and throw him at Elliot. I kept my arms by my side. "The kid's back with her parents," I told him. "It's all over."

He snorted. "All over. Hell, it ain't hardly started yet." I studied him, trying to make out the face to compare it with the photographs of terrorists and most-wanteds that the R.C.M.P. put out. I couldn't recognize him. I could see that he had a slabby usefulness to his build. He had been a manual worker at one time. There were tiny black pits on his face. I figured he had worked in the coal mines but I couldn't pick out any regional accent—not Nova Scotia nor Alberta nor any of the Yankee states.

He reached out to the kid. "Keep the gun on him, Elliot,

133

but bring it here." Elliot handed it over, never letting the muzzle waver. I had no chance to move. When the older one had the gun he said, "Put your hands on your head, Bennett."

I did it, slowly, wondering why he was using my name. He might have learned it in a briefing before all this began, but in a normal situation like this he would have called me 'pig' or 'copper.' This was almost personal. I wondered why, and how the news could help me.

He told the kid, "Look on his belt, he'll have keys for them cuffs." Elliot took a step toward me but Tom stopped him. "Work from behind him, this is a mean one, this is a real he–eero."

Elliot wasn't smirking now. He came behind me and felt around under my parka until he found the key ring on its chain. I felt the tugging as he uncuffed himself. "Now put them on him. Crank 'em up good, we wouldn't want him getting too comfortable, would we?"

I hoped he would cuff my hands as they lay on top of my head—that would mean I could bring them down in front of me, a tiny advantage, but Tom was too clever for that. "Hands behind you, Bennett," he said.

I lowered them and Elliot snapped the handcuffs over my wrists. I was splaying my fingers, pulling my hands up into my sleeves, but he carefully pulled the sleeves back and clamped the metal on my bare arm tight enough to cut the flesh.

"Done," he said triumphantly. It hurt but I was grateful that he had not cuffed me around something. I would be mobile, at least, handicapped as I was.

"That's good." The dark guy grinned, a humorless parting of his lips, a crinkling of the small amount of skin I could see outside his beard. His eyes stayed cold as the night outside. Now he pushed the gun under his arm as if he was going hunting. I weighed the odds. It would give me an extra second but I needed more. He was eight feet away and I was slowed by the handcuffs, they pulled my shoulders back and dulled my edge. I knew he would step back a pace if I moved and cover me, perhaps even shoot. I had to wait for a better chance. I needed a clear kick, at least.

He reached behind him for a chair and sat down, gun on his knees, looking at me. "You don't remember me, do you?"

"Should I?"

"Yeah. I think you should. You cost me six years of my life, you know that?"

I fed his face through my memory again. How many men have I sent to prison? How many of them looked like this man had, years earlier?

"Six years. In Millhaven, mostly. And that ain't no summer camp, you know that."

Now I remembered. My heart thumped hard. Millhaven, Canada's toughest maximum-security prison. Tom? Tom Burfoot. He grabbed ten years on an extortion charge. Extortion, nothing. It had been a dynamiting group. The year I joined the Toronto Police Department after three with the Marines. They put me undercover, infiltrating a group that had started up to copycat the successes the F.L.Q. had scored in Quebec. They had claimed they were revolutionaries, but that story was a scam. They were booked for straight violence, bombing restaurants and movie houses to collect money for their cause. None of the money was recovered. Tom had spent most of it on vacations and on betting at the track. They had been very skillful. Their bombs were dirty, filled with scrap metal and soaked in oil to tattoo survivors forever with black scars. Fortunately only one of the bombs had been set while people were in the restaurant. Only one man had been wounded seriously, the owner. He lived his last few years in a wheelchair, fewer years than this man had spent inside.

"Yes, I remember you."

"Ever been in Millhaven?" He asked it casually. I shook my head. The longer he talked, the looser he would be, the more chance I might have to rush him.

"Yeah. It's where they put the bad-asses, all of them. There's a bunch of bikers in there. They hang together, run the drugs, hand out the punks."

There was nothing to say. He went on, rambling. "Hell of a place. Looks like a furniture factory from outside. Inside, it was the worst place in the world." He looked over at Elliot and grinned the same cold grin. "You would've dug it, Elliot. Five, ten guys takin' turns."

Elliot lowered his eyes and said nothing. Tom turned back to me. "I was lucky. I guess I looked mean, a little ugly even. Nobody wanted me real bad." He cleared his throat and spat on the carpet. "An' if you didn't go for that stuff, nothin'. No tail for six stinkin' years." His anger was building. "No women. So when I got out I had me some catchin' up to do."

I glanced at Elliot. He was flushing. I guessed that he and Tom were lovers. Or that was his reading. To Tom, Elliot was just another object for casual sex, a vehicle for the tastes he had built up during his six years, tastes he still didn't want to talk about. I fed him a question.

"How come you killed a good thing like that Katie? Way I hear it she was crazy for you."

He snapped alert. "Who said I killed Katie? That wasn't me. That was Nighswander."

"Yeah, well, the room was in his name, I know that."

He grinned again. "Cool, eh? I bring the broad up here an' she books the room using his name, like I told her."

"And he killed her for that?"

He spat again. "No. He killed her for me. He was jealous of her. He figured I wouldn't want him no more once I got hold of her."

"You kick with either foot?"

136

He snorted. "After six years in Millhaven you take what's there. Men, women, I don't care." He said it proudly, the vicious, biker's pride in shocking normal sensibilities. He didn't know that my capacity for being shocked was long since overloaded and burned out.

"So is that how come you beat his head in when you found him in the cottage on the island?"

He looked at me for perhaps half a minute. Then he laughed. "Hell, why not? You ain't going nowhere. What's to lose? Yeah. I found him there, where he couldn't do his pantywaist kickin' an' flickin' and I asked him about the broad and he said what happened an' I pounded him one or two with a log."

"Hear that, Elliot? That's what happens to old boyfriends on this circuit." I spoke to the kid but he still looked down at the floor, flushed and humiliated. If throwing a tantrum would help me get free, I could count on him. Otherwise I was still alone except for Valerie, and she seemed frozen with fear. I did not dare look at her, I didn't want to remind Tom of her presence.

I had no need to. He spoke again. "So, anyway, big shot. You know why I came up here?"

"No, Tom. I don't." Lull him, soften him, get him off guard. Maybe Val would make a grab for the gun. She didn't even have to reach it. All I needed was a clear kick. Two seconds!

"Tom!" he said jeeringly. "That's nice. You wanna be friends again. Kiss an' make up, right?"

I said nothing and he swung around suddenly, pointing the gun at Val. "I came up here because I was gonna get at you, an' I know the best way." I looked at Val. Her face had shriveled. She was frozen with fear. I knew she could not help me.

He turned back to me, smiling again from the cheekbones down. He came a little closer, but still out of range of a leg sweep. And he still had the gun in both hands, ready to aim and fire.

"You know what I'm gonna do? Big shot?"

He moved still another step toward me. His hatred was boiling up. I wondered how I could stoke it further, make him concentrate on me first. Then Val would have a chance, we both would. I'd been in places as bad as this before.

"I know you're a big-mouthed dip-stick and you'll talk it up first, whatever it is," I said, trying to sound bored.

It worked. A muscle jumped at the corner of his eye and he clenched his hands on the gun. "You think so? Is that what you think? Well, you'll see what I'm gonna do. I'm gonna bang this broad right here on the rug where you can watch. You made me miss a lotta tail. Now I'm gonna cut me a piece of yours. And when I'm done, Elliot can have her."

I did not look at Valerie. Her fear filled the room like white sound. She was helpless with fright.

"You're a gear box," I sneered. "You don't go for women. You ball punks like this one, pretty little Elliot with his dyed hair."

Elliot gasped with shock and strode toward me, but again he didn't take the final vital step in front of me. He stood off to one side and threw a light punch at the side of my head. I ducked and it grazed the top of my crazy, burned leather hat.

Tom said, "You'll see. You'll see if I'm a gear box. I've been saving this one. I could've screwed her an hour ago but I didn't. I wanted you watching."

"Takes you that long to get it up, does it?" It was working. Both of them were angry. Foam was balling in the corners of Tom's mouth. I spat at him. It didn't quite reach, but it angered him and he lost the rest of his control. He glared at me for a few seconds, then told Elliot, "Undo his belt and pull his pants down."

The kid jumped to do it. He was chuckling. I guess he

thought there was some kind of sexual indignity to the action but I knew better. It's an old gypsy trick. With my pants around my ankles I couldn't kick, couldn't run. I would be immobilized.

I was right. When my heavy uniform trousers slid down past my knees, Tom turned and laid down the gun across the chair. He came up within arm's length of me, beyond the reach of my hampered feet. Without saying anything he slapped me, slamming my head left to right, right to left, perhaps a dozen times. It jangled my brain, but the leather cap saved my eardrums and I was able to keep control. "Still think I'm a faggot?" he asked, breathing heavily. He was out of shape. In a fair fight I could take him.

"Right." I spat again. It was the only thing to do. It might give Val the impetus she needed to go for the gun. If she did, we could win. Tom was the only one to fear. But she stayed on the couch, hunched back on it, making herself as small as she could.

"Tough guy," he said and slapped me again, but more contemptuously. It was lighter, easier to bear.

"You're a jailhouse punk," I told him. "I'll bet you put out for candy bars."

That hurt him. He stepped in and slammed his knee at my groin, but I anticipated and turned. He bumped my thigh but not hard enough to paralyze the leg. And then, as he drew back his knee to try again, I head-smashed him full on the nose with my forehead. I knew it would buy me no more than a second. I ducked and grabbed the waistband of my pants, straightened up, legs free again, and swung a clean kick up between his legs into the testicles. He groaned and doubled over and I kneed him in the face, then turned on the kid. He backed off, holding his hands in front of him fearfully, but I roared the way that Parris Island instructor had taught me and followed him into the corner, kicking him in both knees. I was wearing heavy padded skidoo boots.

A soldier would have ignored the kicks but he collapsed, more afraid than hurt, and I stamped on his left shin for good measure.

I didn't wait any longer. As I turned I could see Tom clawing for the shotgun and I covered the ground in two strides, putting the third stride into a kick square in his abdomen. He oomphed and fell backward, gagging for air. I sat down on the gun and shouted to Valerie, "Quick, unlock me. The key is on my belt."

She came alive at last, trembling and slow, far slower than I wanted, but she found the key still on its chain on my belt and unlocked me and I clipped one cuff over Tom's wrist I rolled him onto his face and twisted the arm up his back. Then I turned and called the kid. "You, get here." He came like a whipped puppy, trembling, stooping to rub his shins. I cuffed him to his partner and then stood all the way up, opening my parka so I could tuck my shirt in and zip up my pants and fasten my belt.

Valerie was weeping helplessly and I held her for a moment, patting her on the back. "It's okay, Val, don't cry. You did well, we beat them." She still sobbed and my mind left the room and the present and raced in pursuit of the other two women. Where had they gone? How had they gotten there? What were they doing? They were the only missing pieces in the whole puzzle. With them in place, I could take Valerie back home and soothe her, slowly, calmly. She stopped sobbing, a sudden, conscious strength that made her straighten up and draw in her chin. "That's right," I told her. "It's all over. Don't worry any more."

I patted her a few times more until I could feel her straighten up, picking up the slack in her body. Then I let go of her shoulders. "Sit down a minute and then we'll go. I just have to talk to this kid."

She sat down and I bent to look Elliot in the face. He was sitting with his legs out straight in front of him, staring into the middle distance. He looked like a runner who has just finished a marathon without placing in the money. "Where did the two women go?"

He didn't answer, didn't appear to notice me. I snapped my fingers in front of him and he shook himself like an animal and looked at me. "The two women, Rachael and Margaret, where did they go?"

He sighed heavily, as if the air were thick and it was an effort to take it up. I told him, "Look, I'm not interested in your Mickey Mouse little slap at me. The only charges against you are for being involved in this plot to kidnap the girl. Tell me what you can and I'll do what I can for you at the trial." He looked at me through wide eyes and I went on with the part of the story he wanted to hear. "If you help me, you won't go to jail, you won't have to go through the kind of stuff Tom talks about."

That turned him on like a light. "They said they had business to finish." He paused for a moment. "I asked them where and they wouldn't say."

"They must have said something, given you some kind of hint."

Tom was beginning to stir. He tried to move but collapsed again, holding his stomach. I didn't know if he was injured. Even in the moment I was kicking him, I had been a policeman, not a Marine. Had I wanted, I could have killed him, but I had drawn the kick marginally, winding him rather than crushing his internal organs completely. I guessed he would be able to move within an hour. I was glad he was handcuffed to Elliot. He wouldn't go anywhere dragging the kid.

Elliot scrubbed his hair with the flat of his hand. "They didn't say much of anything."

"All right, try it another way. How did they get clothes to leave? I took all their parkas with me."

"When Tom came, he lent Margaret his parka and she

141

went to another cottage and broke in and got clothes for her and Rachael. And she came back and said there was a skidoo there. Tom went and hot-wired it for her and brought it back."

"That means they had clothes and a machine. What did they say to one another when they went?"

Elliot looked at me, into my eyes, with an innocent, pleased grin. "I remember. Rachael was laughing. She said to Margaret, 'Come on, old lady, put on your dancing shoes and we'll go.' "

I stood up, grinning with him. "Well, I'm damned. They've gone back to the dance."

15

I didn't crouch forward on my ride back to the station. I sat like a tired tourist, with Val behind me hanging on around my waist. She was still in shock, and to get her talking I asked her about the station. What had happened that Sam hadn't worked his customary protective trick? She explained that Tom had knocked at the back door. Sam barked at him and he had called out through the door that he had the girl with him, she had to be gotten inside out of the snow, she was cold. Too cold to speak, he said, and had pretended to try to persuade her. Val had been hesitant about opening the door but he had reminded her that Sam would protect her, this was an act of mercy, she had to open up. And when she did, he came in gently and calmly with a live grenade in his hand. He had warned her that if Sam attacked him they would all die. The two prisoners had screamed and she had been afraid and finally she had done what he asked and put Sam in the cell.

The girl from the Legion had offered to go with Tom, anxious to get back into the action, but Tom had told her, "Stay here. You can't do as much good as this one can," and had taken Val with him. She had struggled, but he hit her a couple of times and she gave up.

I listened, nodding back over my shoulder but wondering what had happened to the grenade. I had searched the clothes of the two men before we left them in their prison cottage, but they could have hidden a grenade anywhere in the place and I wouldn't have uncovered it without a metal detector. Perhaps Margaret and her last disciple had taken it with them to the Legion. This thing wasn't over yet. It wouldn't be until I had those two women in my cozy little bucket. I was tired enough to grin at the pun, a whole cell in my two cells.

I decided to go first to the station. I could leave Val there and go on alone to the Legion. If that was where the women had gone, it was the only danger spot in town. She would be safe at the station even without Sam. I planned to put him in the skidoo trailer and pack him with me.

I didn't mention any of this to Val. Instead, I nodded a lot and reached back once or twice to hold her arm. And I pointed out that the snowstorm was slowing down, the worst was over now, the wind had dropped, and what snow was still coming down had no viciousness to it, it was like a scene out of Dickens.

Sam barked when we got back to the station but stopped at once when I whistled reassurance. I stood for a moment, enjoying the silence of the night for the first time. With the wind calm, the air seemed almost warm and there was no sound but the pinging of the engine of the snow machine as it cooled. I knew the skies would clear by morning and we would have a perfect picture-postcard day, clean as the birth of the world, while I tied up all the paperwork and gathered up the bodies tonight had left scattered. I almost forgot about the two women and my mission at the Legion Hall.

We went in and Sam bounded up to me and I fussed him and Valerie let the Carmichael girl out of her cell. And I filled the coffee pot with water. Val shucked her coat, not

144

speaking, and set about making the coffee while I sat for a moment, rubbing Sam's ears and working out what to do first. I decided to check the Legion. I phoned but there was no answer, the busy signal buzzed and buzzed in my ear. Probably the line was down, or snow had blown into one of the external connections and shorted the circuit. I swore mildly and put it down.

Almost immediately it rang. I looked around at Nancy Carmichael. "Has it rung much while I've been out?

"I didn't hear it. Not once."

I picked up the phone. "Police Department, Chief Bennett."

The voice was high and old and frightened. "Come at once, there's a dead man on the stairs."

I almost laughed. "If you're calling from the Lakeside Tavern, I know about it. Who's speaking, and where are you?"

"Carmichael, at the Tavern. How do you mean, you know about it?"

"I put the sonofabitch there. He's the guy who kidnapped your daughter. She's here now. She's safe." I didn't say safe and sound. She wasn't sound, not in her own mind, anyway. It would take months, perhaps years of therapy before she reconciled herself to what had happened and her own part in causing it. As a policeman, I'm lucky. I just pick up the pieces. Other people have to put them together again.

"Can I speak to her?"

"I'll ask her." I turned to Nancy, who was leaning against the corner of a desk. She looked vague, detached. "It's your father, Nancy. Can you talk to him?"

She looked out of sky-blue eyes for an eternity. Then she reached out her hand for the telephone.

I did the tactful thing, went back out to the space by the cells where the coffee was perking briskly. Val followed me, moving as if she were eighty years old. "Want some?"

She nodded. "Thank you."

"There's mugs under the counter out front and I've got some brandy in the stationery cupboard. I think a slug of that would help." I went and fetched them, carefully not listening to what Nancy was saying to her father. It seemed for the most part to be single words, followed by long pauses while that thin, old-man's squeak came out of the earpiece. "There's coffee when you're ready," I told her. "No cookies, but I might be able to find you one of Sam's dog biscuits if you like." I winked at her and left. I didn't like what the phone call was doing. It sounded to me as if her father was unloading a parcel of blame. That wouldn't help anything, least of all her attitude.

Val poured the coffee and I slopped in some brandy. Just for her. I had one more call to make and I wanted to be as sharp as I could manage. If the Sumner woman had a grenade with her, anything could happen.

Nancy came back out as we were sipping and listening to the two prisoners ask very politely if they could have coffee, too.

"My father wants to speak to you," she said. I nodded and gestured to the coffee. "Have some, it will warm you up."

I could hear Carmichael speaking to someone else at the other end so I said, "Bennett here," in a businesslike voice and waited. At the other end he was telling somebody to wait upstairs, but she wouldn't. I imagined it must be the Iron Butterfly he had married. Then he spoke into the phone.

I was expecting a thank-you speech for saving his daughter, but he was too important to waste time on trifles like that.

"Bennett. Good. I wanted to talk to you."

"What's on your mind?" I didn't feel polite. My job involves keeping the peace in this backwater and except for his daughter's involvement in this crazy scheme I would

146

have been in bed for five hours now. Instead I had been shot at, slapped, had my girl threatened with rape, and been obliged to kill a man. Just in the line of work, but it didn't make me very tractable.

"She said there was a woman called Margaret involved in this plan of hers."

"Yes, Margaret Sumner, maybe fifty-five, one-forty, around five foot four. Looks as if she might be an Indian."

"Is that her married name?"

That made me think. I hadn't noticed any wedding ring, but then, we hadn't met at a cocktail party. I'd been busy.

"I'm not sure. It's not an Indian name that I've heard in any of the bands up this way."

"Fifty-five, you say?" He was nervous. When he spoke to me first he had been scared, angry, but now he was nervous. His voice had the metallic tingle of tense people, heart attack candidates. And this was not much to do with his daughter, this seemed more personal.

"Around fifty-five. You know how it is with Indian people, they don't shrivel up like city folks. But they don't have face lifts, you have to guess. I'd say from fifty-two to fifty-eight would be right. Why are you asking?"

He cleared his throat, an unpleasant dry rasp in my ear.

"Well, thing is, I wasn't always in industry. I started out after the war in geology."

Save it for your memoirs! My mind was racing ahead, hurdling over the dribs and drabs of life story he was going to send my way. The fact was he knew this Margaret, or somebody very much like her. And from the sound of his voice, she had no reason to love, honor, or respect him.

"Look, I don't have time for all the details. Are you telling me that you know somebody who might fit this description?"

His voice rose in alarm, which he masked as indignation. "Now don't go jumping to conclusions."

"I am not prying into your private life. I'm just putting two and two together and coming up with sixteen. From what I read you used to work in the north, you knew a girl who would be the age of this Margaret. Is that right?"

He coughed again, like somebody easing the bolt on an old Lee Enfield rifle. "Yes. You could say that."

"And what was her name?"

A long sigh. "Her name was Peggy. Peggy Burfoot."

Burfoot! I felt a shock of understanding race up my arms from the fingertips and into my brain. I almost shouted at him "Burfoot? Did she have a baby? Would this have been back around nineteen forty-seven, forty-eight?"

"I don't know about any baby." He whispered it. I guessed his wife was standing over him.

"Don't jerk me around. This is important. Did you leave her knocked up back a couple of years after the war?"

Again the sigh. Bless me officer for I have sinned. "It's possible. I lost track of her. I moved away, down to Montreal."

And meanwhile a frightened, pretty Indian kid found herself pregnant. Her father would have been ready to kill her. He would have thrown her out. She would have headed for Toronto and had the baby, a black-haired, bright-eyed little bastard that nobody wanted. Those were the days when babies were a dime a dozen. People were marrying and moving to new suburbs and having three kids each. The baby would have been shunted from one foster home to another. By the time he was six or so the other kids would have started slapping him down and calling him a half-breed. I could see the whole pitiful pattern, the thefts, the sadness, the punishment, the bigger crimes, the penitentiary I had put him into. I felt humbled. If the nickel mine stope had collapsed on my father when I was eighteen months instead of eighteen years old, this could have been almost my story.

148

At last I said, "Mr. Carmichael. I think I've met your son. Why don't you get yourself a double shot of brandy out of the bar and settle down? I'll call you back later."

There was no answer and after an eternity the phone went down, as gently as the snow that was still falling outside the window.

I replaced the receiver and sat on the edge of the table. You can't afford to be sentimental as a policeman. Kind, yes. Merciful, compassionate, but never sentimental. The child Carmichael had abandoned was dead and buried under thirty-five years of grief and change. The man who had replaced it was pinioned in a snowbound cottage. I was only glad I had pulled that kick.

Valerie said, "What's the matter? You look terrible."

I tried a grin. "Old age, kiddo. This is a young man's occupation and I feel about ninety."

She smiled at me nervously. "It's not that bad," she said, but she didn't come over to me and put her arms around me the way she would have done eight hours before, when the world was a warmer, happier place. I could sense that I had lost her somewhere along the trails I had covered this night.

"I'll be fine. Maybe I'll have a touch of that brandy before I go."

"Go where?" Her voice rose in horror. "You're not going anywhere else, surely not?"

"I have to close the circle, tell the folks at the Legion that everything is all right." It wasn't the whole truth but I wasn't sure how much more she could handle. "I'll be back in half an hour. I'd phone but the line must be down."

Her voice was harsh. "You don't have to go out and do any more. Nobody expects that of you."

"Just my boss," I said, and explained what I meant by flipping one cocky thumb at myself. "Me."

16

I prepared for the trip to the Legion as carefully as I would have done for a night patrol in Nam. Not with armaments. I knew I would be better off with my handgun than the shotgun. You can't use buckshot when there are civilians around, it spreads into a cloud that cuts through the air like grapeshot from Napoleon's cannons. I needed a clean, single shot, if I had to fire at all. But I was hoping it wouldn't come down to violence. It usually doesn't, even when you're up against men. Unless these two women were dedicated terrorists, they wouldn't fight.

The first thing I did was to check the address book I maintain in the office. It gave me Margaret Sumner's permanent address—or it should have. All the other property owners in the area have their names and addresses and phone numbers listed with me in case someone breaks into their place and I have to contact them in an emergency. But Margaret Sumner had no telephone number. I could now remember making the entry last summer when she bought the place. She gave me a post office box number in Toronto, no phone. In an explanatory P.S. I had added the note, "Travels extensively, cannot be reached quickly."

So that was one blank. I had nowhere to send the Toronto police to cover. I did the next thing I could. I separated the two prisoners and brought Freddie into the front office to talk to me. She came gladly. After talking to Nancy Carmichael and learning that I had shot the man at the Tavern, she realized that there are other sides to my character than guardian angel. And she had probably spent a lot of her time in the cell thinking about how close she had been to death.

As I brought her out the other girl snapped at her, "Don't help him. He's the enemy." I figured that humiliating herself at the Legion had stoked up her own personal hatred of men. She was useless to my investigation. But Freddie took no notice of her.

"What is it you want to know?" Her voice was neutral but there was tension to it. She was wondering if I was going to be harsh. I wasn't, anyway, but I had no need to be. I had the advantage that interrogators like to build up. It had happened for me accidentally but I knew it would work. She was still wearing the clumsy clothes I had brought her out on the ice. Their shapelessness made her feel incomplete and foolish, but their presence reminded her of what I had done. She had unzipped the parka in the warmth of the station, but she sat now clenching it together with both hands.

"To start with, why did you unload my gun? It could have gotten me killed."

She didn't answer. She looked at me, then lowered her eyes and shrugged one shoulder nervously. She spoke softly after a while, not raising her head. "I'm sorry. I didn't think you needed it. I thought it was just a symbol of—you know—masculinity. Emptying it was a kind of a joke."

Good guys versus clowns one more time, I thought. I was the blustering sexual cliché, she was the wise woman of the world. I wondered whether I should bring her up to date on everything that had happened since our encounter on the ice, but I didn't bother. I sat and looked at her without speaking. I could see her eyes were brimming with tears. She was like a child found playing some dangerous prank, not knowing how close to death she had been. It seemed to me that she had silently changed sides over the last couple of hours. The reality of the cold out there on the ice had convinced her that C.L.A.W. didn't make any sense. My help when her life depended on it had washed away her ability to believe the jargon of any ideology. I figured she was ready to help me, to make amends. So I asked her my questions.

"I'm going to the Legion Hall. I have reason to believe that Margaret and the woman you call Rachael have gone there, planning some kind of disturbance. Before I go, I want to know anything you can tell me that will help me to deal with Margaret."

"But I thought you'd met her." Her head came up again and she looked at me shyly.

"I need to know her attitudes, her point of view, anything that will help another policeman arrest her if she gets away."

She thought for a moment, changing her grip on the front of her parka.

"I need help *now*," I reminded her softly. "If you can't help, I have to get up there. They have a grenade with them and that hall is full of people."

She started. "You don't think they'd use it?"

"One man's been killed with one already. Think quickly."

"There isn't much to tell. But it did seem to me that she was educated and proud of it."

"Why do you say that?"

"She quoted a lot." Freddie paused and waved one hand, pushing her hair back with the other, but it was an unconscious gesture—she was working for me. "I mean, she would give us examples of what she meant and then she would always tell us who had said it. That was part of the thrill of being involved with her. She made us feel special, particularly intelligent and educated."

"Examples like what? Marx, that kind of stuff?"

152

"Oh yes, him of course, but not just jargon. Like she gave us, when one of the girls was wavering, a long speech about everybody who is with us, the magistrate who hesitates to give the maximum sentence because of being afraid of looking reactionary, and so on and so on. And then she told us it was from some Russian, not Tolstoy . . ."

"Dostoyevsky, *The Possessed*," I said. That made her look up again in sudden respect. "Do you think she was a professor somewhere?"

"She might be." Freddie pushed her hair back, and the gesture seemed to clear not only her face but her memory. "That's right. She said once, 'I tell my students,' whatever it was."

"And did you meet at odd times or always on weekends?"

She gave a little bemused laugh. "You ask the strangest questions."

"Think." I needed answers, I had to leave my life insurance package with Valerie before I went, the information that would convince Margaret not to pull the pin on that grenade.

"It was through the week, weekends, any time, no pattern."

"Thank you." I stood up. "What about Rachael?"

"She's a total mystery. She never said anything except in answer to questions or to applaud Margaret sometimes."

"Okay. I have to lock you up again. I'm sorry, but I appreciate your help."

She stood up now, gracefully, both knees together, every inch the model. "It's mutual, you know. I know what could have happened to me on the ice."

"Let's not get into that. When you emptied my gun you could have gotten me killed. I'd prefer to forget that end of our acquaintance." I ushered her to the back again and locked her back in her cell. The other woman hissed at her, "Lackey."

I gave Valerie a nod and she followed me out front. "This

Margaret could be a political science professor, perhaps only a schoolteacher, but she must live or work within driving distance of Toronto."

Valerie looked at me dumbly. I reached out and patted her shoulder. "I want you to make a note of that. If anything goes wrong at the Legion and she gets away, that's the information you give to the OPP investigators."

"If anything goes wrong?" She looked as if she could weep. "Reid, what could go wrong?"

"If she isn't there, or gets away before I get there and the OPP call. That's what you tell them. That's all. Her name is Margaret Sumner, she is an Indian, and her maiden name was Burfoot. That should give them enough to go on."

"But you'll tell them." Her eyes were wide. "I don't want you getting hurt, you'll tell them, won't you?"

"I'll have no need to. I'm going down there to arrest her right now. Meantime, you're in charge. I'm taking Sam, but I'll leave you the shotgun and there's a can of Mace. If anyone tries to get in, spray that in their face."

She was pale to start with but in that moment she whitened even more. I tried to reassure her. "Nobody will. The women are at the Legion and the only male members of the outfit are handcuffed together a mile away from here."

"You didn't see if they had a skidoo?" The thought must have been preying on her—she blurted it out, then looked away.

"No need to worry, they can't get apart and the kid can't get dressed so they won't be going anywhere even if Tom ever gets his wind back." I winked at her and turned away. Dammit. I should have immobilized that skidoo. It was just simple common sense, but I hadn't done it. I'd been too busy soothing Val.

I didn't wait any longer. Sam came when I whistled and I took him out and connected up my little sled behind the skidoo. He jumped in on command and I left for my last chore of the night, a security check. That was all it would be, if I was to have any luck at all this night.

There was a time when I would have rushed up there and burst in. But tonight I was a policeman, not a Marine, and I wasn't going there to kill anybody, even Margaret. I was there to carry out my sworn oath, to protect life and property and maintain the Queen's peace. I wondered how to do it best.

There were a couple of choices, neither one practical. One was to try and sneak in through a window so I would have the drop on anyone causing mischief. That would have worked in a house, but the Legion was the standard northern Ontario social hall, built to keep out the cold. The windows were small and high and double-glazed. The door behind the stage was another option, but it was locked. Somebody would have to press the crush bar on the inside or I'd have to use an axe. No. Subtlety was out. I would walk in the front door with my gun in my right hand, half drawn, and my stick up my left sleeve. Sam would come with me. If anything was going down, he would help defuse it for me.

So that's what I did. The snow had drifted across the front door of the hall, but it was trampled where somebody had entered within the last hour. I prepared both weapons, called Sam after me, and went in. I was quiet, but anybody inside would have heard my snow machine. There would be no surprise.

The lobby was empty and there was no sound, no music, no talking or laughing. I pushed the door open and went in, Sam like a shadow at my heel.

The hall was full of people all sitting on the floor, legs crossed, facing the stage. Women were weeping silently and men were trying to soothe them. And on the stage sat Margaret Sumner with Rachael next to her holding a shotgun on Walter Puckrin, who was standing in front of the stage.

Rachael looked at me when I came in, flashed a quick look at Margaret, then back at me. But she didn't level the gun at me. If she had, I would have shot her, taking the chance on beating her to the reflexive action on the trigger, but I couldn't do that when it was a civilian who would be at risk. Fifty feet is chancy range for a revolver. I would need two seconds to aim and fire. In that time Puckrin would be dead. So instead I ambled forward, moving around the edge of the crowd, keeping myself isolated in case she did swing the gun toward me. I moved clumsily, the big dopey copper ready to trip over his own feet, a joke. If she would only relax long enough to laugh at me I could take her. She didn't laugh, didn't speak. It was Margaret Sumner who told me, "Put your hands on your head, Bennett."

I shrugged, let the gun slide back into the holster, and did as she said, but Margaret was onto me. "I know your gun is in your right-hand pocket. Take it out very carefully with your fingertips and drop it."

"Jeeze, Margaret, have a heart. I'm supposed to be a symbol to these people, how does this make me look?" Lesson one in hostage negotiations, don't let the person with the hostages build themselves a line of action. Whenever you can, change the subject, keep them wondering what you're talking about. Obey, if you must, but don't go along with everything unquestioningly.

"No more talk. The fat man dies if you screw around." She was cool, unimpressed. I took the gun out and lowered it to the floor, then pushed it with my toe away under the stage where nobody could reach it without crawling for twenty feet on hands and knees.

"Can't just drop it, it might go off," I said. Then before she could repeat her warning I said, "Oh, sorry. No more talking."

I had my hands up and I kept coming. The stick was still up my sleeve. The right swing of my arm would send it cartwheeling at Rachael. She would raise her arms to protect her head and I would have my two seconds to close in. If Margaret didn't have that grenade.

Margaret said, "Make your dog lie down, then sit and put your hands on your head."

I stroked Sam's head. "Down. Good boy." He obeyed, but he whined in his throat. He could smell the fear around him. He knew he was needed. He was baffled.

I turned back to Margaret. "I prefer to stand up. I've been on and off that damn snow machine all night."

She almost lost her cool. "I said sit!" she snapped, but I shrugged. "Gimme a break. I'm saddle sore." I was ten yards from the gun. If I could close to five I could win. Once I sat, the chance was gone. At last she shrugged. "So stand."

I was at one side of the hall. There were about eight couples sitting on the floor in the line between me and the woman with the gun. That had to change. Whoever got killed tonight, I would be the one blamed. After the arrests were made and the inquests held and Margaret and Rachael put in the Women's Penitentiary at Kingston, people would still go over what had happened here tonight and they would come back to blaming me. I was responsible for enough deaths. I didn't want any more at my door.

Margaret was watching me, still making up her mind whether to force me to sit. I spoke to her, my voice totally serious now. "Can we have a word in private?"

"I don't want to hear you talk any more," she said. Her face was as rigid as a Roman emperor's. In another minute she would turn her thumb down and Rachael would swing the gun around on me and it would be all over.

"I have a personal message for you."

"From whom?" Maybe an English professor, not political science, I thought.

"You wouldn't want me to say, not in front of all these people. Her eyes narrowed and I inched forward another pace.

"I know your background, Bennett. You're supposed to be

157

resourceful and dangerous. I'm sure you've spent hours in classrooms preparing for scenes like this one. Just shut up and sit down or my friend here will pull the trigger on the fat man."

Walter Puckrin looked around at me. He said nothing, but he was afraid. It was forty years since he had won his medal, fighting against straightforward, businesslike enemies whose job it was to kill. He didn't understand this generation. He had learned their techniques from the TV news and he knew they had pulled triggers on people a lot more valuable or pitiable than he was. I looked back at him and then to Margaret.

"Please. My message is from Tom's father."

For a moment I thought I would have my chance at Rachael. The barrel of the gun wavered as she flicked her head around to look at me. I figured she was putting her own two and two together and wondering at the new architecture her group had developed since Margaret first approached her. I wondered if she would be disenchanted suddenly, if she might turn the gun on her leader instead of a bystander. But she turned back to stare at Puckrin with the old unflinching gaze. My country, right or wrong, my leader, single or married.

Margaret took her time before speaking. "You have no message. You have no knowledge. But I am beginning to believe you have seen a certain member of my group and I hope, for your sake, that he is well."

"Fine. Just fine." The right tone, apologetic, the response to someone who has trodden on your foot and is making polite inquiries. "The person I'm talking about is a former geologist, related to another person in your organization." All around me people were turning to one another, wondering what I was talking about. And wondering why I wasn't acting like a TV S.W.A.T. team, blowing people away from the muzzles of guns instead of talking to them in a rational tone of voice.

Margaret said, "You have a very active imagination. I'll grant you that. I guess you spend a lot of time watching TV."

I didn't mind the sneer. She was loosening, becoming personal when she should have been detached and distant. Insults were a crack in the wall. With work I could chip a hole big enough to climb through.

"TV, eh? Try this plot on for size. Young war hero comes out of college in the forties. Comes north to a place so remote you can get there only by float plane or canoe. Stays for a summer and starts romancing a local girl." She said nothing, but it seemed to me that some of the stiffness in her back and neck was softening out. She was listening.

"How am I doing so far? Anyway, hero is called back south and leaves a problem behind him."

She snapped, addressing Rachael, not me. "Keep that man covered. I have to talk."

She bent, put one hand flat on the stage, and slipped gracefully down to my level. She pointed at me. "You. Put your hands on your head and turn to face that wall."

This time I complied. It would make it next to impossible for me to swing and grab her, making her a shield and turning this scene into a Mexican stand-off. I didn't think Rachael would shoot while her leader was menaced. And I would menace her. I know holds that could snap her neck like a carrot. I turned, dutifully, standing two feet from the wall with room enough to swing around. But she was ready for that move. "Nose and toes to the wall."

I did it, moving in slowly. There was a crack in the plaster and it ran north and south through my consciousness, as raw as the Grand Canyon.

"Now." She said it very softly, from a couple of feet behind me. "I'll hear that message."

I ran through all the possibilities. It was like playing chess in a blindfold. I didn't know which pieces were important or what the reaction would be. I had to make this count. It was the last card in the hand.

"He was in tears." I let that dangle, but there was no reaction. I invented as quickly as I could, but kept my voice calm, just the messenger. "He was sent to Brazil. He got down to Montreal and they sent him off at once. He thought he was coming back up north again but instead they sent him overseas and when he got back it was too late to do anything. He wants to see you. He'd lost all track of you, and now he wants to see you."

This got a reaction. "And how does he propose to do that, with that blonde bombshell he's married to hanging around? What's she—number three, is it? Number four?"

I turned my head slightly and when she said nothing I turned my whole body to face her. I could see Rachael, over her head, still pointing that shotgun at Walter Puckrin, but watching us jealously. That was the emotion in her face. She loved this woman and I was certain in that moment that she would fire the shotgun as fast as she could pump new rounds into the chamber. I had to cool her out.

"He was in tears. And I don't think he's a man who does much crying. He wanted you to know that his life has been miserable."

There were many angry, vicious responses possible but she did not make them. She looked at me and said, "Miserable? How does he think his son has been? Foster homes, prison. Miserable! He doesn't know the meaning of the word. Misery to him is not making money fast enough, not laying the pretty girls fast enough, not drinking the good cognac and smoking the Havana cigars. He's miserable about things most people never even get to dream about."

My chances were improving. I could feel it. All I needed was time and quiet so I could be the sympathetic, understanding friend. People don't menace friends with shotguns. Soon the gun would be lowered and the menace would be over. Given time and a never-failing gift of gab.

"Your own life has been successful. You're an educated woman. You've got money. You're a credit to yourself."

"To my people," she corrected ironically. "That's the proper degree of patronage. As if an Indian were somehow incapable of being educated, especially when she starts off at the Salvation Army Grace hospital with a white man's baby in her belly and no money."

"I'm not patronizing you. I haven't lifted myself the way you did and I had all the breaks an Indian boy wouldn't have had. My father had a good job with INCO, I finished high school."

She looked at me unblinkingly. "You could have done it. You're tough enough to be Indian."

"I've had to be tough, but not that tough. I settled for three square meals a day and the uniform."

"Were there any Indians in the Marines?" It was an honest question and I was able to lower my arms as I answered. She was beginning to trust me. I was afraid she might wonder about her son. If she suspected I had put him down in a fight, had injured him and left him handcuffed, all this human interest, hearts and flowers mood would flash away like magnesium and turn into a white heat that would leave her capable of killing me. I had to tread a line to get some concessions now.

"One Pima, in my platoon. He lived through it. Last time I talked to any of the guys I heard he was running a gas station in New Mexico." All lies. He had come home in a body bag, what we found of him. I held out my hands pleadingly. "Margaret, these people here are frightened. Why don't you let them go?"

Her expression did not change but it seemed that the light in her eyes became less bright. "Have you been telling me the truth?"

"Every word. But I'm worried about these dumb people. The civilians. They don't know where anything's coming from. Turn them loose."

Rachael must have heard me, perhaps even read my lips, I swear my voice was no louder than a whisper. She shouted suddenly, "Don't listen to him. Action on behalf of women, that's why we're here."

I grabbed it, any reaction was better than nothing. "Fine, then. Let the women go. Keep the men, that emphasizes your point. Why don't you do that?"

Margaret looked at me a long time. I felt like the prisoner waiting for the judge to pronounce sentence. Would it be a year, life, or a dismissal? At last she spoke, calling out loud enough for all the people in the hall to hear. "The women may leave. No men. Just the women."

The hall broke out in a babble of talk. Rachael's voice rose over all of it, shrill, bitter. "It's a trick. Don't trust him." Margaret locked her eyes on mine, uncertain, wavering for a moment, and I took my cue. "No tricks. Women only, prove your point. I'll help you."

She nodded and I whistled, Sam at once sprang to his feet, and all the people turned to look at me. Not all of them stopped talking but I shouted, "Women only. This lady says the women can go and that's the way it has to be. The women take their coats from the cloakroom and go and sit in your cars. Take the car keys and start the engines so you won't freeze. But no men."

The women got up, unfolding like flowers in their party dresses. One young woman hung onto her husband's arm. She was sobbing and when I reached her I could see she was pregnant. I went over to her and told her, "It's all right, he'll be out in a few minutes." The husband looked at me, then licked his lips nervously and told her, "Go, Corinne. Take care of him." He touched her stomach gently. Their love hung in the air like honeysuckle. "Good girl," I told her. "Your husband won't be long."

Close to the back of the hall a man jumped to his feet and ran for the door. Rachael shouted and I kept my promise. "Track," I called, and Sam ran between his legs and tripped him, then stood over him snarling. I went over and told Sam

"Easy." He relaxed and I patted his head. The man still lay there. He had wet himself but I made no comment. "Women only," I said. "The rest of us are going to wait a while." I held out my hand to him and he got up, ignoring my hand, and went to the center of the room, not looking at anybody. His wife shrieked at me, "You bastard!" but I ignored her and went back to stand close by Margaret, part of the new establishment.

A lot of the women were sobbing, but it didn't stop them from getting their boots and coats on. Many of them had drunk too much during the evening but they were all cold sober now. I stood and watched them. "Don't try to drive away, the road is blocked to anything but snow machines. Start your cars, stay warm, stay awake."

The men watched as their own women left, then turned to look at me, some with resignation, some with blazing hatred in their faces, but they said nothing. They would remember their own danger long after they had forgotten their wives' safety.

When the last woman had left I moved away from Margaret, drifting slowly closer to the stage. Rachael was still standing, still holding the gun on Walter Puckrin, but the strain was beginning to tell. She had probably never carried a gun for any length of time. Now she was finding that it was a machine, and like all machines it was heavy. I knew already. I'd carried my M16 over more klicks of jungle than she had ever seen. Her arms were trembling. I hoped she would keep her finger off the trigger. She turned and looked at me and her arms tightened convulsively. "No closer," she told me.

"Would you like a chair?" Just a thought. If she was green enough to accept I could sweep her feet away, throwing the gun barrel up at the ceiling. It would be all over without blood.

"Chauvinist swine." She hissed it. I shrugged.

"You sure do take all this personally, Rachael." I hoped it would widen the gap I'd pushed between her and Margaret, but Margaret's mood had changed already. She knew she had been outmaneuvered and was hiding her anger.

"Sit down, Bennett. I mean it," she said. And this time I sat. There was nothing to do for a few minutes anyway, until it was time to make the next exchange, when her mood had settled again. I had recognized the town's lawyer among the men. Soon I would suggest that he help draft her demands. If she had any demands. So far she had said nothing. But she must have a real purpose for doing this.

I let her go for three minutes before I asked her, "Mrs. Sumner, can you let us know what you want in return for the safe release of these people? I assume your League has some specific political aims."

She didn't like my tone. "You've talked enough. I'll give you my demands when we get the attention I need outside."

"That won't be for hours, maybe a full day."

"I have all the time in the world."

"Do you want to talk to the man I spoke to you about?" I hoped not. If he told her anything different from what I had invented, she would probably tell Rachael to pull the trigger on me. She did not answer and I didn't press it. I sat waiting for the boredom to begin to build. Most hostage situations devolve to that at some point. It is the eventual undoing of all the cases that end happily for the hostages.

She went back to the stage and sat on the edge of it. Then she called Rachael over, and Rachael came, keeping the gun on Puckrin the whole time. They changed over. Margaret took the gun, balancing it over her knees, pointing at Puckrin. She was smart, I knew that. If she were an amateur she would point at me, but Puckrin was a better hostage. His death would disturb more people than the death of a copper. And his life was vital to me. If he died, I would be blamed for killing him.

We all sat still. Outside I heard cars starting up, revving high as drivers rushed the heating system to protect themselves from the cold that would be intensified by their fears for their own safety and the safety of their menfolk.

And then, far off but coming closer, as pure as an ascending glissando on some electronic instrument, I could make out the whine of a snow machine. I checked my watch. It was four forty-three. Nobody would be moving at this hour unless they had some special reason for coming here. And to confirm my thoughts, the note bent like a harmonica sound as the machine pulled into the parking lot and right up against the front steps.

Everybody in the room craned around as the outer door closed with a hollow boom. Then the inner door opened and a man stood there, one hand clutched to his stomach. For an instant I didn't recognize him in his tight, green workman's parka, then I saw the handcuff dangling from his right wrist in the same second that Margaret's voice gave a half scream. "Tom! What's happened to you?"

17

He came into the room slowly, walking straddle-legged around his injured testicles. He had heavy leather work gloves on, and as he took them off I could see that his right hand was rusty as if he had dipped it in paint. And the empty half of my handcuffs still dangled from it.

"Ask him," he said in a low, hoarse voice. He came through the crowd of seated men and stood a few feet from me. I willed Sam not to growl and he didn't, his training too deep to presume in my presence.

"Wondering how I got away? Is that it, tough guy?" He held up his right hand so I could see it better. I could see that the rust was turning to black and I knew what had happened. "Easy," he said, and laughed with a sound like the bark of an angry dog. "Easy. You didn't look around that cabin too good, did you? There was a hatchet in the kindling box. I disconnected the kid."

"You cut his hand off?" I could hardly believe it. I knew he was a killer, but that kind of deliberate horror was too hard to imagine.

"Don't worry about him none. He won't be needin' it. You

worry about you." He held out his left hand and I saw what was in it. "See this? Know what it is? It's a grenade. Seen one before?"

I had seen, and used, dozens of them. It was an M67, a fragmentation grenade, capable of killing most of the people in the hall. If he was careful and went out to the doorway he could bounce it in among us, then drop flat below the stone step that rose to this level. He would live. We would die, or suffer injuries most of the men in this room had never dreamed of. Only the Legion veterans knew what grenades can do.

I noticed he had already removed the safety clip. Now he removed the pin, keeping his hand clamped around the lever. He tossed the pin casually among the people on the floor and they scrambled away from it, all except for one gray-haired man who looked at it without flinching.

"If you killed the kid that makes four people you've wasted tonight."

He laughed again, stopping in mid-bark as pain struck his diaphragm. He coughed gently, clutching the hand with the grenade to his solar plexus. Then he straightened. "You've done better than that in your time," he said. "Women, kids, no problem to our big tough Marine."

I glanced at Margaret Sumner. She was sitting mesmerized on the edge of the stage, her mouth slightly open. The gun was slumped upside down across her knees, the muzzle pointing harmlessly up at a spot high on the side wall. This was the break I'd prayed for earlier, but now it was too late. Her son had us much more secure than her single-hit gun ever did.

I was willing her to shoot him. If she did, I could have a chance to grab the grenade before he dropped it, before the lever flipped away and the last four seconds of our lives began to tick. But if I was too late, I was helpless. There were heavy drapes over the window. I would not have time to part them, smash the glass, and throw the grenade out. And if I

167

did, I had the new problem of my own making. The parking lot was full of women sitting behind the eggshell security of their Detroit sheet metal. The fragments would slice through three of them in a row. I would have dead women on my hands.

But otherwise? Otherwise, what? I would die here, among a number of others. I had to negotiate.

"Margaret, talk to him. He's your son, he'll listen to you. Tell him not to let go of that thing, I'll put the pin back in."

Tom waved his left hand, pushing out his lower lip and making a downturned smile. "I'm through takin' orders, Bennett. And so are you." He jerked his head to the women on stage. "Come on, you two. Out in the lobby an' lay down. I wanna open these guys' Christmas present."

Margaret slid down, holding the gun in one hand by the barrel. Then Rachael followed. She had lost her anger but none of her hatred. She sneered at me without speaking as she passed.

Tom waited for them to go to the door, then followed slowly, painfully. I had caused him pain. So far that was the best news I had had all night. We all swiveled our heads to watch him go. He stood at the door and addressed us all. "Any of you wanna say a prayer, get it said." He paused to give another painful cough. "On'y make it quick. This here is a capitalist weapon, same as your hero used in Viet Nam. When I pitch it in, you're on your last four seconds. It will kill most of you like a lot of people got killed in that rotten war. Any of you as don't die, I'll come back for."

My head was racing. Around me men were weeping, praying, some pushing themselves back, vainly, on hands and heels. I knew I had to load the dice my way if I could. I broke in on his speech.

"Don't listen to this punk. He's nothing more than a jailhouse queen acting butch."

He pointed at me with his right hand. "You sent me in there, you sonofabitch. I was straight as an arrow up to then."

168

"Gearbox!" I roared it. "The only way you can bang anything is with a grenade."

It worked. Instead of tossing the grenade he hurled it directly at me, hard as a line drive in baseball, hard as the hockey slap-shots I used to grab out of the air when I played goal for Sudbury my last year in high school. I was ready. It was all slowed down as if I were on dope. The lever catapulted away in a series of slow lazy loops. I counted in my head, the seconds booming like cannons.

One! Grab the grenade out of the air, swinging my arm back and spinning completely around to take the force without shocking the load any further.

Two! Shout "Fight" to Sam, who jumped for Margaret Sumner who was struggling to bring the gun up to a firing position while her son pushed her toward the lobby door and I leaped toward the door of Puckrin's office, dodging the flat bodies of men who groveled there, willing themselves smaller.

Three! Into the office and over the desk.

Four! Roll the grenade into the open safe with my right hand and slam the door with my left.

I hit the floor as the grenade exploded, muffled by the walls of the safe but loud enough to deafen me. Without pausing, I shook my head and came back into the hall on the run in case Sam had failed to pin Margaret Sumner.

She was tugging back against his jaws clamped on her right arm, trying to reach the trigger with her left hand. Tom was looming over and around her, punching at Sam. Sam was ignoring him, snarling, holding, ignoring the punches. Then as I sprinted toward them, I saw Tom making a dagger of his thumb and stab down, going for Sam's eyes. I let out a roar of fury and drove right into him, smashing him up under the chin with the edge of my left hand.

He flew backward and I turned and punched Margaret in the abdomen, a clean, short click of a punch that doubled her over and let the gun clatter to the floor. Rachael was cowering back, covering her eyes with her hands. I pointed to her and told Sam "Keep" and he jumped in front of her, snarling, poised to leap.

I glanced at Tom but he was out of it, clutching his throat, gagging, dying. I knelt and patted his pockets—they were empty—then his mother's. She lay looking up at me sightlessly, and then her breath came back in a long, howling whoop.

I stood up. I was trembling all over. In that second I could have wept, but slowly, one breath at a time, I calmed myself and stood looking down at Tom, who was going blue in the face. Then I felt the first man at my elbow. I turned and recognized Dr. McQuaig. He said nothing, just dropped to his knees beside Tom. "Quick. Your knife," he commanded. I took out my clasp knife, black from the smoke of the chimney of hours, years before when I had straddled the roof of the cottage. He opened it, pausing to wipe the blade on the front of his shirt, and made a small incision in Tom's throat. Blood welled out and the doctor shouted, "Quick, a ballpoint pen."

I was too stunned to move but he shouted it again and someone ran up holding a pen. He unscrewed the body and tossed aside the mechanism, then crooked his finger around the exposed windpipe, slit it, and inserted the tapered end of the tube into the slit. Tom kicked and tried to grab it but the doctor held his hands. "Leave it alone and ye'll live," he shouted. Then to me, "Bennett, hold his hands."

I took one, Walter Puckrin took the other, and the doctor sat on his legs and slowly Tom's kicking subsided and air whistled in through the pen body. His color came back. The doctor looked at me and grinned.

"Haven't seen so much excitement since the day we landed in Normandy," he said. Other men came in to take over holding Tom and we all stood up. The doctor retrieved my knife from the floor, wiped the blade on his handkerchief, and said in a voice as Scotch and clear as Irv Whiteside's beloved J & B, "I believe the rascal will live."

170

"Thanks, Doc." I reached out and shook his hand and as we shook he added, "Y'know, there are times when I wish I weren't quite so damn handy at m'job."

Slowly it was all put back together. Men went out and brought the women back into the Hall. Other men took turns holding Tom's hands and feet while the doctor supervised. Me, I took off my burnt, itchy leather hat and went to the bar. Men were clustering about me, banging me on the back, trying to shake my hands. I was the King. I was the guy who had saved their lives, made good triumph over evil, and most important of all, given most of them the only exciting memory they would ever have. All of which would be forgotten the first time I had to write them a summons for failing to come to a complete stop at the stop sign on the highway.

The barman pushed the bottle of Black Velvet at me, with a tall glass. I poured myself a solid drink and took a good long pull on it. I nodded my thanks and walked over to Sam, who was watching both the women. Margaret had her breath back by now and Rachael was sitting with her knees drawn up and her hands over her face. I ignored them both and stooped to fuss Sam, tickling him under his good ear and telling him he was a good boy.

And then I hear a sudden angry bellow behind me. Moving on reflexes I stood up, holding my glass low, ready to pitch it at the face of the man if he attacked me. I saw Walter Puckrin striding toward me. His face was black as thunder but he was laughing as he came.

"You crazy, dangerous bastard," he roared. "You know what you just did?"

"I saved a bunch of asses," I said. Modesty was taking second place to truth now I had taken a good taste of my rye.

"That's just the half of it." He held up his hands and trickled out a cloud of scorched confetti. "You just blew eight hundred and ninety-three dollars to rat shit."

18

We saved Elliot. Dr. McQuaig had his bag in his car. Norah Puckrin had been a nurse in the naval hospital at Halifax during the war so the kid was lucky enough to get two knowledgeable people with all the training needed to care for wounds like his. We all took off down to the cottage on a fleet of snowmobiles and stormed in. The room looked like a slaughterhouse, but Elliot's arm was sealed with a tourniquet. He was moaning, but the bleeding had been stopped almost immediately.

"He didn't put this on himself," the doctor said. He was filling a needle with morphine as he talked, his neat gray suit smeared with Elliot's blood. "The bastard who cut his arm off must have done this."

I left the doctor to it while I relit the stove and got other men to fill the log box and bring blankets from the bedroom. Norah made sweet tea for Elliot and McQuaig pumped him full of antibiotics and gave him a tetanus shot and checked the tourniquet again. Elliot screamed for a while but the morphine took over and he drowsed off. I looked at the tourniquet. It was a good piece of bush-worker's first aid. A nylon sock had been tied loosely over the end of the stump

172

and a piece of kindling pushed through it and twisted until the blood flow stopped altogether. Tom must have done it, using the skills he had learned in some pulp-cutting camp where injuries are a way of life.

We left a couple of men there, with Norah, to keep the stove going and to take care of the kid when he came around. The rest of us backtracked my night's adventure, examining the bodies of Irv Whiteside and the man I'd shot and the dead girl at the motel. It was too much for the other men. Most of them dropped out of the party after looking at Irv. Others when we went to the Lakeside Tavern and they saw the boy who'd tried to kill me. He was older than Elliot and tougher in appearance. But he was cold dead, and one of the men threw up at the sight. It was too much, after holding everything in at the sight of Irv Whiteside.

Just the doctor and I went to the motel. By then it was daylight. The snow had stopped and as we came out of the cabin the first car came south.

"If the snowplow is working again, it's time to get Burfoot and that boy Elliot to the hospital. I've taken no more than rudimentary care," McQuaig said. "They're in no shape to travel but the boy canna stay where he is."

We went into the office and used Fred Wales's phone to call the OPP. They sent the helicopter. It came to the motel and lifted me to the cabin site. One of the men said he would take me back to the station so I stayed behind, watching the helicopter take off, swirling the snow around us in a cold, bitter cloud, a black and white replay of all those times in Nam.

When I got back to the station, I thanked the driver. He yawned and nodded and went away up the road to the Legion Hall to pick up his wife and take her back to their cottage. I watched him go, thinking how I envied him. I still had paperwork to do and no doubt there would be reporters to talk to. Then, perhaps by noon if I was lucky, I could go back to my place and join Val. I planned to have her dropped down there by the first vehicle that came by.

I walked to the front door of the station, stepping high over the drifted snow, and opened the door. Val was inside, in front of the counter, smoking a cigarette. I hadn't known she smoked. Her coat was lying across the top of the counter and she was wearing her outdoor boots. Carmichael, his wife, and Nancy were all sitting in the front office. The wife was smoking and I guessed that was where Val had picked up the habit again. They all turned and looked at me wearily, too tired to ask anything. I nodded to the Carmichaels and said to Val, "Are you okay?"

She nodded three or four times, as if she were trying to convince herself. "Yes," she said at last.

"There's nothing for you to do here. I'll get you dropped at my place and come down later to join you once the nonsense is all finished. Charges, reports, you know."

"I know," she said, but there was no life in her voice. She might have been talking to a stranger. She turned away to stub her cigarette, searching for an ashtray.

"The floor's fine," I told her gently.

She dropped the butt lifelessly and ground it out under her right foot. The Carmichaels were watching us. I knew the cells were still full of prisoners so I took Val's arm. "Put your coat on and step outside a moment, please."

She put her coat over her shoulders, not bothering to slip her arms into the sleeves, and came with me back into the bright sunshine that was flashing blue lights out of the new snow. She blinked at the light but did not turn her head from the sun or put up her hand to shield her eyes.

"You look beat, honey." I was tired down to my bones but I wanted to give her all my spare energy, to turn her back into the glowing woman who had come up to me at the dance in the Legion such a long time ago. Behind us there was the grinding roar of a heavy vehicle. I turned and glanced up the road toward the Legion. A big gravel truck with a plowblade in front was coming toward us slowly, arcing a high wing of snow off to one side of the road. I watched until it drew level with the station and the driver waved to me ingratiatingly. I waved back, recognizing Cassidy, rested after a good night's sleep, earning extra money by clearing the township's roads. He looked eager to please and I watched him until he had passed, showering us with a fine mist of dry crystals of snow. Then I turned back to Val. A veil of crystals had settled on her hair and they were melting, glinting ruby and emerald in the morning sun. She was beautiful.

"Reid," she began, then stopped. I said nothing. I've seen this kind of shock a lot of times. It's fragile. One word can shatter it into tears. "I don't know what to say," she said at last and raised and flopped her arms, helplessly.

"Look, you've had a hell of a night. You've been threat-ened, cut, seen a whole lot of bad stuff. Don't say anything."

She gathered her strength, drawing in a long breath and holding it until she gasped. "It's more than that," she said at last. "It's like it was with Bob, all over again."

She tried to say more but failed. She looked down at the snow and kicked one foot absently, puffing up a small cloud. I didn't touch her. I knew what was going on inside her head. The scab over her husband's death had been almost healed. She had begun to laugh again. She had had the courage to come north to meet a replacement—me. I wasn't fair-haired and funny like Bob, but I was a solid man who was ready to take on a new family and teach the boys to fish and swim and cross-country ski and do all the things their father had started when they were tiny. And I loved her. We both knew it, but we'd never used that word—you don't, until all the old ghosts are put away. And now she was starting to under-stand again what a policeman does, what he is, and she wasn't sure she could handle it.

After a long while I said, "Don't think about it, I'll get you back to the Legion to pick up your car and you can head for home. Stop somewhere soon and sleep, it'll help."

With the first hint of firmness she said, "I don't think I can sleep, not without being at home with the boys, knowing they're safe."

I reached out and touched her hand lightly. "Drive carefully." She pursed her lips and nodded once or twice, then said, "You're a good man, Reid Bennett."

"Yeah. Look, maybe next month I'll be in Toronto again. I'll come by and we can take the kids to a movie or the museum or skating—something."

Now she looked up at me, and the corners of her eyes were sparkling with the same brightness as the crystals in her hair. "They'd like that," she said.

I put one arm around her shoulders and squeezed gently, then led her back into the station and helped her off with her coat. She sat down on the recycled church pew I have against the wall in front of the counter and I walked away through the little half-door to the main office.

I sat down at my desk and picked up the telephone. My life as a man was in ruins, but I was still a copper. I had work to do. I phoned the magistrate and asked him to come to the station for a bail hearing on the prisoners. I asked him to drive by way of the Legion and have somebody escort the two women down with him. That way I could finish with all of them at once.

Then it was time to talk to Carmichael. I asked his wife and Nancy to wait out in the back of the station. The wife wasn't happy, but Carmichael looked at her out of plaintive hound-dog eyes and she went. I sat looking at him for a minute before speaking. He was pale and sick but he spoke first.

"What happens with Nancy?"

"Nothing. As far as I'm concerned she was a victim, not

a member of the conspiracy." I had already planned what I was going to do. I would charge the two C.L.A.W. members with public mischief. The two who had held the hostages were in bigger trouble. So was Tom, but there was no need to include all the women in the same mess, it could complicate things for me and I wasn't out for blood. I'd already had as much as I could stomach.

He looked at me and cleared his throat harshly. "What about the attack on Nancy?"

"The man who did that is dead. If you say nothing, the whole business can be kept quiet. Nobody will know but Nancy, your wife, and you."

He thought about that for a moment, staring down at the toe of his boot. At last he cleared his treacherous throat again and nodded. "Yes. That would be best."

That was it. No thanks. No recognition of the fact that I was cutting corners for him. But I've been a copper too long to worry about that. I stood up. "Now the plow's been by, why don't you take your family and go? Nancy should at least be checked out by a doctor."

He didn't straighten up, kept staring down at the floor as he said softly, "I can't work out what happened."

"You were in the middle of it," I told him. "I guess Peggy Burfoot's group had planned to hold you hostage and get some kind of concession from you—maybe money, maybe something to do with the U.S. rocket work your company's doing. They had it set up with Tom and his crowd. He waited at the cottage down the lake until I turned up, then he went on to the Legion to join his mother."

Now he looked up. "What cottage?" I glanced across at Val but she had given up worrying. She had curled on the pew and closed her eyes. She may even have been sleeping. Briefly I told him what had happened. He listened and then shook his head silently. I nodded at him and went out back.

His wife and daughter were drinking coffee. They had

given each of the prisoners a cup. I told the Carmichael women they could go back out front and then I let the prisoners out of their cell. "The magistrate's on his way. When he gets here you'll have to answer some questions and then you'll be free to go. I'm charging you with mischief for your part in last night's kidnapping."

The thin one said nothing. Freddie laughed, a nervous laugh but still musical. It was the first real laugh I'd heard in twelve hours. "Feeling generous, Chief?"

"Not really. Just tired." I shooed them through to the front of the station and sat down at the little table to get my thoughts in order for my report. In a minute or so I picked up the clipboard and began to scribble. I heard the Carmichaels leaving to walk back to the Lakeside Tavern, and a few moments later I heard the magistrate arrive. I went through to the front office to greet him. He had the two women from the Legion, along with Sam and a couple of hung-over Legionnaires. I stooped to fuss Sam, who was delighted to see me and wagging his tail almost off his body. The Legionnaires left and I set up the formal bail hearings. On my say-so, the magistrate released the two younger women on their own recognizance but remanded Peggie Burfoot and Rachael for trial. I put them into the cells and called the OPP to send out a policewoman escort to take them to the Regional detention center.

The magistrate left, happy to be escorted by the three women, Val, and the two younger C.L.A.W. members. I had to find some shoes for Freddie, an old pair of skidoo boots that must have belonged to some former chief. Val lingered after the others had gone out into the snow. She tried a bright little smile and it almost worked. "Don't you give up on me, Reid. I need time, that's all."

I smiled back, even though I could see it wasn't true. She could never come back here. Every night would have been filled with terror. Tom Burfoot had done what he had set out to do. He had demolished a corner of my life, the most important corner.

"I'll be here when you're ready," I told her. She craned up on tiptoe and kissed me on the lips, a quick, dry, sisterly kiss. A good-bye kiss. Then she was gone.

I went over to the typewriter and wound in an occurrence form. It was the only thing to do. I was only halfway down the first sheet thirty minutes later when the door opened again and Freddie walked in. She had dressed, presumably in spare clothes from her car, blue jeans and a sweater under her parka. She was awkward, swinging her legs slowly and holding her face very tight. She looked as tough as a girl that pretty can look.

"What's up, forget your purse?"

She lifted the flap on the counter and walked through to my side. "No," she said defiantly. "I just figured I'd caused you enough trouble and I came to say I'm sorry."

"You're forgiven. Go home."

She came over to the typewriter and looked over my shoulder at the half page I'd finished. She snorted. "A good job I did come back. I'm no stenographer, but I have to be ten times better than that. Let me see the machine a minute."

I stood up and she slipped into the seat, pulling out the sheet of paper I had so painfully typed. Then she took her coat off and began to type in crisp bunches of sound, like the clatter of an M16 on full automatic. Within a couple of minutes she stopped. "Okay, now dictate the rest, I want to see how it comes out."

I sat down across the desk from her. "You mean you'll type the whole thing?"

"Like I told you," she said roughly, "I owe you."

19

Freddie stayed a month before she got home-sick for the bright lights of Toronto. By that time the trial had started and the publicity she got for having appeared nude on the ice was enough to get her a couple of decent TV appearances. Then there were the talk shows, and soon she had outgrown both the feminist movement and me.

I stayed where I was, of course. I liked Murphy's Harbour. The town was good to me. They held a roast for me at the Legion Hall and ended up locking me in my own cells on a charge of laughing too hard. It was all very small town and corny and it covered up the embarrassment people feel at knowing you have saved lives, their lives, while they were too paralyzed with fear to know what was going on. Carmichael died within that month. His heart gave out on the night before the trial began. But he had done a couple of gracious things. He had paid for the damages to Carl Simmonds's house. He made a two-grand donation to the Legion. And he hired a sonofabitch of a tough lawyer for his son Tom and for the two women.

That was where the fun all stopped. The story came out bit by bit under the probing of our local Crown Attorney.

It was no wonder Margaret Sumner hated policemen. A year earlier her husband had been killed by a car that was being pursued by the Montreal police. It happened the night he retired. He was older than she and had sold out his real estate partnership and taken the money. The two of them were going to Europe the next day. Then they would have returned to Mexico and the circuit of the wealthy retired set. She would have studied ruins and he would have played golf and gotten browner and browner. But fate stepped in and slammed their car broadside as they were on their way home from the retirement party.

Sumner had died the following day. His widow buried him and contained her anger. She made an attempt to overcome it by hiring a detective to trace her illegitimate son. They found Tom just finishing his six years in Millhaven— a sour, silent, angry con. That blew away the last of her resilience. She wanted to hurt the people who had hurt her. That included Carmichael and the policemen who embodied all her reason for hatred. Tom was glad to take part. He'd spent six years of solitary nights dreaming of getting back at me. So she set up a plot that would humiliate and torment Carmichael and kill me. It was a vendetta, but she was clever enough to try to put a barrier between herself and the crimes she wanted to commit. She created C.L.A.W. and conned Nancy into joining. I don't think the rape was intended. Sumner was too much of a feminist to go along with further suffering of any woman. But she used her people well.

They had whisked Nancy away from the dance. They were going to take her to the Sumner place on the island but gave up that idea when they found Whiteside there. Instead they took her to the mainland, leaving Nighswander in the cottage close to the fishing huts in case I should go there, and later leaving Elliot at the end of the crack in the ice. I was marked for death one way or the other.

But Tom's ferocity spoiled the plan. He wanted more than

my death. He wanted me to suffer and he picked Val as the instrument. By then the whole crew of them, C.L.A.W. members, Tom's friends, everybody, was so caught up with the excitement that they'd thrown their plans away. They decided to go to the Legion and hold Carmichael hostage. That's why Tom came down there after he severed the kid's arm. He was ready to be Hitler, Attila, anybody with the power of life and death over a bunch of terrified hostages. The way the Crown Attorney summed it up was, "They were drunk on blood."

Only I got lucky and caught that grenade in time. The jury sat stone faced and listened to the whole story and found the three principals guilty. Tom was sentenced to life in Penetanguishene, the hospital for the criminally insane. The way the Act is written, he's there on a Governor General's warrant, but in fact he was to be there forever, he was beyond rehabilitation. His mother and Rachael were remanded for sentence. Margaret was released on bail, pending an appeal, and she disappeared.

I don't think they tried very hard to find her. She was too important a symbol. She had beaten the odds on her own. Starting a week after giving up her baby she had put herself through school, through college, and into some American university. She was a credit to the whole Indian people and this crazy blot on her copybook could have ended that. So she walked.

And I walked, back to Murphy's Harbour, to lengthening days, to summonses to the owners of ice-fishing huts for not pulling their places off the ice early enough, to looking up at the first crows of February, and the returning ducks and geese of April, to a way of life that was beginning to suit me more and more. Who can tell, I may stay here until retirement. Me and Sam.